英语战争诗歌选

张宏伟 陈韵姿
石佳凝 陈洁
徐艳萍 编译
参译

陕西师范大学出版总社 西安

图书代号　WX24N2291

图书在版编目（CIP）数据

英语战争诗歌选 / 徐艳萍编译. -- 西安：陕西师范大学出版总社有限公司, 2024. 12. -- ISBN 978-7-5695-4801-3

I. I12

中国国家版本馆CIP数据核字第2024Y290Y9号

英语战争诗歌选
YINGYU ZHANZHENG SHIGE XUAN

徐艳萍　编译

出 版 人	刘东风
责任编辑	焦　凌　扈梦秋
责任校对	刘　定
封面设计	ONEbook
出版发行	陕西师范大学出版总社
	（西安市长安南路199号　邮编710062）
网　　址	http://www.snupg.com
印　　刷	中煤地西安地图制印有限公司
开　　本	880 mm×1230 mm　1/32
印　　张	12.5
字　　数	297千
版　　次	2024年12月第1版
印　　次	2024年12月第1次印刷
书　　号	ISBN 978-7-5695-4801-3
定　　价	58.00元

读者购书、书店添货或发现印装质量问题，请与本公司营销部联系、调换。
电话：（029）85307864　85303629　传真：（029）85303879

《哈里·帕奇之死》《政权更迭》已获得版权方 The Wylie Agency (UK) Limited 授权。Copyright©Andrew Motion,used by permission of The Wylie Agency(UK)limited.

大卫·克里格诗歌已得到其遗孀出版授权。

译者序

最早的战争难以查考，似乎有了人类，就有了战争。

早在公元前近9000年，生活在约旦河谷杰里科的人们就曾建起一座令人敬畏的塔。但很多考古学家对这座塔的军事功能存疑。考古学家在号称最古老的城镇巴勒斯坦的杰里科城和今伊拉克的乌鲁克城发现了最早的战争实据——公元前7000年前用以防御的城墙。公元前4300年建立于今土耳其梅尔辛的高墙被认为是防御工事。之后，西亚的防御工事屡见不鲜。最早的关于战争的壁画可追溯到公元前3500年的基什王国。公元前3100年，苏美尔（今伊拉克南部）的乌鲁克城就有了一道令人叹为观止的9.66千米（6英里）长的城墙。但是修建这道城墙的居民的定居点却被摧毁了。这说明，就在人们拥有了足够的组织能力修建防御工事的同时，也拥有了足够的组织能力来攻克这样的防御工事。

有历史记载的最早的战争爆发于公元前2700年的美索不达米亚。贾雷德·戴蒙德在他的经典研究成果《枪炮、病菌与钢铁》中说，农业的发展提升了人口密度，人们找到了更多打仗的理由。人类几乎会为能想象到的任何事情相互杀戮。从古至今，虽然战争的缘由迥异，用柏拉图的话就是，为了满足自身的欲望，人需要财富，对财富的追求导致了战争，一切战争都与财富的攫取有关。

有了战争，后有了关于战争的诗歌。史上记载的最早的战争诗歌是来自苏美尔月神庙女祭司、女诗人恩赫杜安娜（苏美尔国王萨尔贡的女儿，被认为是世界上已知最早的作者）在公元前2300年抒写的怒斥战争的诗歌：

你是从山上奔泻而下的鲜血
是仇恨、狂怒与贪欲
天地的主宰

古希腊诗人荷马的著名史诗《伊利亚特》写的就是长达10年的吞噬众多生灵的特洛伊战争。这场战争摧毁了勇士的魂魄，使他们的身体成为腐肉，成为野狗们与群鸟的盛宴。

最早的英语战争诗歌是公元991年一个匿名的盎格鲁·撒克逊人用古英语描述"马尔登战役"中武士们挥刀舞剑、奋力拼杀的英勇场面。莎士比亚曾这样描写战场："有的咒天骂地，有的喊军医，有的哭他抛下的苦命的妻，有的抱怨未还的债，有的呼唤他苦命的孩"——死在战场上的人，尊严尽失！事实上，不少杰出的英语诗人创作了关于战争的诗歌，英国桂冠诗人骚塞、任职最久的桂冠诗人丁尼生、第一位获得诺贝尔文学奖的英国作家吉卜林、对英国文学产生深远影响的著名小说家及诗人哈代、获得诺贝尔文学奖的爱尔兰诗人叶芝、"悖论王子"切斯特顿及人称"疯狂的狄兰"的狄兰·托马斯和意象派运动的发起人庞德等都用自己的笔墨抒写战争或对战争的看法。譬如，当大多数英国人都支持布尔战争时，托马斯·哈代却逆向而行，用诗歌表达他的反战思想。他在诗歌《他杀掉的那个人》中写道：

战争的确古怪离奇
使你向另一个人射击
倘若酒吧相遇
你会与他举杯畅饮

历时4年多，造成900万士兵阵亡，500万平民死亡的第一次世界大战促生了英国文学史上一个特殊的诗人群体——战争诗人——他们既是战士，也是诗人，他们利用战时空闲通过笔墨记录自己的所见所闻，抒发所思所想。战争诗人这个群体、战争诗歌这个体裁由此诞生。英语战争诗歌主要指受第一次世界大战影响而创作的诗歌。英国桂冠诗人华兹华斯说诗歌是强烈感情的自然流露，同样，战争诗歌抒发战士（诗人）面对死亡时的大义凛然或恐惧，对胜利与和平的渴望，对战争的厌恶等。最著名的战争诗人有威尔弗雷德·欧文、查尔斯·汉密尔顿·索利、鲁伯特·布鲁克、西格弗里德·萨松、艾萨克·罗森伯格、爱德华·托马斯（即菲利普·爱德华·托马斯）等。著名的战争诗歌广为传颂，有的还被谱曲。

战争诗歌主要表达两个主题：一是讴歌英雄主义、爱国主义；另一是揭露战争的残酷，认为"战争是地狱"（出自英国诗人罗伯特·格雷夫斯的诗）或"战争是祸根"（出自战争诗人西格弗里德·萨松的诗），痛斥战争生灵涂炭，悲悯芸芸众生的惨状。

一、弘扬爱国主义、英雄主义的战争诗篇

美国自由诗之父沃尔特·惠特曼的一首短诗《最英勇的士兵》这样写道：

从战场上生还的士兵被冠以盛名——英勇
那勇敢地冲在前方、阵亡的士兵，籍籍无名

任职最久的英国桂冠诗人阿尔弗雷德·丁尼生在诗歌《轻骑兵冲锋》里描述轻骑兵在明知命令有误的情形下恪守军人的职责——服从而非质疑，毅然决然地向前冲锋，最后战死的悲壮故事：

时间怎能湮没英名？
这次勇敢的进攻
举世震惊
致敬，向这次冲锋！
致敬，向这六百名
豪迈轻骑兵！

因《什罗普郡少年》颇受关注的英国诗人A.E.豪斯曼的战争诗歌《我们在此长眠》讴歌阵亡将士的无怨无悔：

我们在此长眠
我们别无选择

要活就会使生养我们的祖国
蒙羞

第一位获得诺贝尔文学奖的英国作家鲁德亚德·吉卜林在一战前是大英帝国热情的吹鼓手。他在爱国主义诗篇《两个加拿大纪念馆》中这样写道：

……
我们从遥远的国度奔赴此地
来拯救我们的荣誉和炮火连天的世界
我们长眠在这异国小镇
请相信，我们为你们赢得了世界！

被诺贝尔文学奖得主、爱尔兰诗人叶芝称为"英伦最英俊的男孩"的鲁伯特·布鲁克于1915年2月随英国地中海远征军出征，因被蚊虫叮咬感染，患上败血症，英年早逝。未亲历血腥战争的他创作的战争诗篇饱含爱国主义、浪漫主义情愫。他的诗歌《士兵》广为流传，人们提及他，必提及他这首代表作。

如果我死了，请如是记住我：
异国他乡的某个角落将永属英格兰
那富饶的土壤里
将蕴含一粒更肥沃的尘土
一粒在英格兰出生、长大，获得心智的尘土

这是一具曾欣赏过英格兰的鲜花，徜徉在英格兰的小径
呼吸过英格兰的空气
接受了家乡河流的洗涤
沐浴过家乡太阳，属于英格兰的身体
……

英国前首相温斯顿·丘吉尔给予鲁伯特极高的评价，说："鲁伯特·布鲁克留下了无与伦比的战争诗歌……这些诗歌是鲁伯特·布鲁克本人全部的历史与写照。"鲁伯特短暂却传奇的一生应验了他的代表作《士兵》里的预言。一战期间，圣保罗大教堂的大主教在圣保罗大教堂宣读了这首《士兵》，并称"再也无法找出更高贵的表达方式来表达纯洁而高尚的爱国主义精神了。"这首诗后来被谱曲，成为名曲。布鲁克的英俊帅气和这首广为传颂的爱国主义诗篇使他成为英国家喻户晓的诗人，甚至有的酒吧以他的名字命名。

每年的11月11日是英联邦国家阵亡将士纪念日，纪念期间，人们献上红色的罂粟花，这一习俗源于加拿大军医约翰·麦克雷的爱国主义诗篇《在佛兰德斯战场》。1915年5月3日，约翰·麦克雷从阵亡士兵的葬礼返回后写下了这样的诗行：

在佛兰德斯战场，一行行
一排排的十字架旁
鲜红的罂粟花随风飘荡
告知世界　我们的鲜血洒在这异地他乡
天空中飞翔的云雀依然勇敢地歌唱

隆隆的枪炮声中听不到它们的歌声嘹亮
我们战死沙场
……
继续战斗吧！从我们垂下的手里
接过火炬，把它高高擎起——
倘若我们的遗志被背弃
纵使罂粟花开遍佛兰德斯
我们也永不安息

这首诗后来在英语世界广为传颂，罂粟花成为英语国家纪念阵亡将士的标志性纪念物。人们在阵亡将士纪念日那天，佩戴人工制作的罂粟花。2016年，英国艺术家手工制作了888,246个鲜红的瓷质罂粟花，纪念一战中阵亡的英军将士。鲜红的罂粟花海"奔涌"在伦敦塔，场面令人震撼、难忘。

一位阵亡士兵墓碑上的爱国主义碑文，迄今依然在英语国家的阵亡将士纪念日的纪念仪式上被诵读：

回家后
请告诉他们我们的故事，告诉他们
为了他们的明天
我们奉献了我们的今天

英国桂冠诗人塞西尔·戴·刘易斯为国际纵队里的英国志愿军写下《志愿军》的颂歌，讴歌他们的英勇无畏：

告诉在英格兰的他们，倘若他们问
是什么让我们参战
让我们来到这高原
在这繁星下的墓地长眠

不是愚昧、不是欺骗
也不为荣耀、复仇或报酬
我们来这里是因为我们睁着的眼
看不到别的出路

再没有别的路可以让
人类摇曳的真理之光永放光芒
……

被誉为"美国的孔子"的美国诗人爱默生在《康科德之歌》中这样写道：

崇高的精神，让英雄们无所畏惧
献身，好让后代享自由

二、批评现实主义的战争诗篇

意气风发的士兵们雄赳赳、气昂昂地奔赴战场，大义凛然地随时准备献出自己年轻的生命，但他们并不了解战争。战争诗人爱德华·托马斯写道：

关于战争的争吵和喧嚣，我并不比风暴中
扫过树林的风了解更多。

获得诺贝尔文学奖的爱尔兰诗人叶芝在他的诗歌《一个爱尔兰飞行员预见了死亡》中写道：

我知道，在那高高的云端
我将结束此生
那些我捍卫的，我不爱
与之交战的，我不恨

这印证了美国诗人兰德尔·贾雷尔（1914—1965）的话，"九成的士兵不知因何而战……"。

哲学家罗素说，人类的灾难可分为两种：一种由自然环境引起，另一种是由他人引起。随着人类在知识和技术上的不断进步，人为的灾难超过了自然界造成的灾难。世界上的文明国家互不相容，互相残杀……（因为多次反战，罗素曾失去过教职、蹲过监狱）。

以下基于批判现实主义理论，分三部分展开。

（一）反映真实的战争

诗人与哲学家一样，是时代的领头羊。他们观察世界的眼光是犀利、冷静甚至残酷的。他们从批判现实主义的不同视角揭示战争的血腥与残酷。

有些诗反映了战时士兵的艰难困境。

许多战争诗人同样是战士，他们亲临战场，饱受战事疾苦，目睹了战争的残酷。艾萨克·罗森伯格是在战争中阵亡的3位重要诗人之一。他参战前长期找不到工作，于1915年10月应征入伍。随部队被派往法国西线的他在战壕里创作了《死人堆》等诸多战争诗歌。他的《战壕里的诗》被公认为是第一次世界大战期间创作的最杰出的诗歌之一。阵亡前他将自己的诗稿寄回英国。

在一封私人信件中他描述了对战争的态度："我从来不是因为爱国的原因参军。什么也不能成为战争的借口……"他的诗《运兵船》着眼于战时籍籍无名士兵们的艰难困境：

荒诞的拥挤
像杂技演员一样地弯曲
昏睡的灵魂
我们以各种方式躺着
却无法入睡
潮湿的风阴冷
蹒跚的人们太粗心
如果你打个盹
风或男人的脚
就会割到你脸上

同样，亲历战争的乔治亚诗歌运动（1910—1936）的领导人之一威尔弗里德·威尔逊·吉布森在战争期间创作了不少优秀的战争诗歌。他的《早餐》描述了战时士兵们窘迫的日常：

我们仰卧着吃早餐

炮弹从头顶呼啸而过

我用一片熏肉赌一块面包

赌赫尔联队将击败哈利法克斯队

当吉米·斯坦索普替换比利·布拉德福德打后卫时

金杰扬起头,接受了赌注,嘴里诅咒着

突然,他倒地,死了

我们仰卧着吃早餐

炮弹从头顶呼啸而过

寥寥数语,将战士们的生活窘境、困境和盘托出。受骑士精神的熏陶,满怀英雄主义情怀,一批批精英志愿奔赴前线。当他们亲临战场时,才体会到战事的艰难。

有些诗反映战争的残酷与血腥。

英国诗人罗伯特·格雷夫斯是英国现实主义诗人、历史小说家、评论家及杰出的翻译家。1914年第一次世界大战爆发后,他应征入伍,在索姆河战役中受伤,与同团的著名战争诗人西格弗里德·萨松一同在牛津大学的萨默维尔学院(当时的军官医院)进行康复治疗,两人缔结了深厚的友谊。他们通过诗歌告知大众战争的真相。他的战争诗歌《死去的波奇》指斥"战争是地狱!"揭露战争的血腥和将士阵亡的惨状:

我要说(或许您早已听过)

"战争是地狱!"如果你们和曾经的我一样怀疑

那么今天，在马梅茨伍德我找到了
对嗜血者的治愈：
我瞧见倚在破碎行李箱上的波奇
死在一堆血糊糊的污秽里
他的前方芳草萋萋
衣物上散发着恶臭，留着短发的他满脸痛苦
戴着眼镜的他大肚子裸露着
污黑的血顺着鼻子和胡须往下滴

曾一度笃信和平主义的英国社会主义政治家、作家和诗人玛格丽特·伊莎贝尔·科尔夫人创作了《老兵》一诗，深刻表现了战争的残酷及表达了她对正值青春年华的伤残士兵的悲怆之情：

见到他时，他正端坐在阳光下
失去双眼的他离开了战场
越过栅栏，一群手捧鲜花的新兵前来拜访
咨询他的战斗经验
他说说这，谈谈那，还给他们讲故事
未提及他脑海里的噩梦
听到我们在旁侧，他说：
"可怜的孩子，他们怎能体悟那绝望？"
目睹端坐着的他
转动着他空空的眼窝
我们中的一个忍不住问："你多大？"

"5月3日刚满十九。"

一战爆发后，正在德国求学的查尔斯·汉密尔顿·索利毅然回国参战，牺牲时年仅20岁。他被桂冠诗人约翰·梅斯菲尔德和战争诗人罗伯特·格雷夫斯等人认为是战争中痛失的最杰出的诗人，他的去世是诗界的巨大损失。《当你看到数百万无嘴的死人》一诗是他阵亡后从他的工具包里找出的。他在诗中这样写道：

当你在梦中看到数百万无嘴的死人
在苍白的阵营里走着
请记着：不要像旁人那样，讲温柔的话语
你不必
也无须赞美他们。他们已经聋了，怎能听到？
怎知道那堆砌在他们炸开的头颅上的赞美不是咒语？
也不要哭。他们失明的眼睛看不见你的泪
也无须授予他们荣誉。荣誉瞬间烟消云散
只说"他们死了。"再补充一句
"之前许多更优秀的也死了。"
……

怀揣为国捐躯的英雄主义梦想，正值青春岁月的他们在一战爆发后毅然决然地奔赴前线。战事的艰辛，战争的残酷是他们始料未及的。持续的战争让更多的士兵丧生。

还有些诗反映战争造成的万劫不复的巨大破坏。

早在1796年，与威廉·华兹华斯和塞缪尔·泰勒·柯勒律治并称为"湖畔诗人"的英国桂冠诗人罗伯特·骚塞就创作了最早的反战诗之一《布连海姆战役后》，揭露战争对平民、士兵及生存环境造成的巨大伤害。

"战火毁了一切，
方圆多少里一片荒凉；
多少母亲和孩子，
在战火中悲惨死去。
你们可知，每场著名战役后，
都是满目疮痍。"
"据说我们虽赢得胜利，
但战后景象却令人神伤，
遍地的尸体，
在烈日下腐烂。
你们可知，每次大胜仗后，
都是这番惨状。"

以疏离淡然的笔调，通过爷孙对话，诗人将胜利的辉煌戳得千疮百孔，揭示无论多么辉煌的胜利对普通民众来说都是一场灾难。无论是对征服者，还是对被征服者，征服的过程并不美好，都会造成尸横遍野、满目疮痍。

英国女诗人伊丽莎白·达里尤什（原名伊丽莎白·布里奇）在《献给美索不达米亚战役的幸存者》中这样写道：

战争毁掉的时代是寸草不生的沙海
经历的人都知道

在毁灭一切的咆哮声中
野秃鹫在盘旋，还有贪欲和卑微的恐惧
那里还潜伏着饥饿、疾病、痛苦
残忍的它们在等待时机
它们将所有生的美丽从一个个肢体上剥离

自愿放弃英国桂冠诗人终身制的桂冠诗人安德鲁·莫伸发表在《卫报》上题为《政权更迭》的反战诗篇讲述战争对文明和历史古迹的巨大破坏，昔日的辉煌因为战争和死亡而万劫不复。莫伸在接受BBC四台的采访时说，这首诗是他的政治宣言，意在"激烈地反战"。谈到伊拉克战争对人类文明和文化遗产万劫不复的破坏，诗人这样写道：

"占领底格里斯河和幼发拉底河
它们曾从童年的画着阳光和沙滩的彩色石板上流过

"今非昔比，我已经用数不清的垃圾粪便
把它们填满

"占领巴比伦，那鲜花盛开的宫殿
……

"如今只剩下顶着星星的尖塔

……"

（二）同情战争阴云下的芸芸众生

有些诗表达对参战者沦为牺牲品的同情。

因其战争诗歌而出名的西格弗里德·萨松1915年底在法国参战。受伤后，给英国陆军部写了一封公开信，拒绝继续战斗。他在信中写道："我认为那些有能力结束这场战争的人在故意延长战争。"在伯特兰·罗素的敦促下，下议院宣读了这封信。玛格丽特·麦克道尔在《文学传记词典》中说，萨松的战争诗歌是"对现实犀利的悲叹或讽刺"。他的战争诗歌《要紧吗？》以讥讽口吻这样写道：

要紧吗——失去一条腿？……
人们都心存善意
当他们狩猎归来
狼吞虎咽地吃下松饼和鸡蛋时
你不必在意

要紧吗——失去了视力？……
有许多盲人能干的活
人们都心存善意
当坐在阳台上的你想起往昔
你可以把脸向光亮转去

……

公众对萨松的诗歌反应激烈，一些读者抱怨诗人缺乏爱国主义精神，还有一些读者认为他对战争现场的描述过于极端，细节过于逼真。《泰晤士报文学增刊》的一位评论家则说，"他的战争诗之所以有活力，是因为在冷嘲热讽的诗行间隐藏着一种强烈的情感。"麦克道尔在《英国诗歌史》写道，"（萨松）之所以被铭记是因为他的100多首战争诗歌。字里行间，他一直反对一战的继续。"

颇受尊敬的战争诗人威尔弗雷德·欧文的死讯（时年25岁）传到他的故乡时，当地的教堂钟声正好宣布战争结束。1985年11月11日阵亡将士纪念日，在威斯敏斯特教堂的诗人角，为投身一战的16位诗人的纪念碑揭幕。碑文是威尔弗雷德·欧文的文字："我的主题是战争和战争的遗憾。我用诗歌表达遗憾。"他的战争诗歌《青春挽歌》正是对与他一样因战争而献出青春的士兵们的真实写照：

什么样的丧钟为那哑畜般惨死的士兵敲响？
唯有那短枪残忍的怒吼
唯有那长枪时断时续的嗒嗒
在重复着它们急促的祈祷

没有颂扬，没有祷告，没有哀悼，没有丧钟
只有子弹刺耳的呼啸声、炮弹疯狂的爆炸声
为他们号啕悲哭

嘹亮的军号声还命令着来自各地的他们奋勇

获得普利策奖的美国诗人萨拉·蒂斯代尔的《战时的春天》抒发了她痛恨战争、悲悯人类的感伤情怀：

总觉春天还很远很远
叶芽的芬芳很淡很淡
春天啊，你怎忍心来到
这悲惨世界
这苦难人间？

战争使诸多血气方刚的年轻人奔赴战场，投向死神的怀抱。英国社会主义政治家、作家和诗人玛格丽特·伊莎贝尔·科尔夫人的诗行喟叹凋零的青春：

正值青春飞扬的他们
却如同飘落在佛兰德粘土上的雪花

有的诗表达对军属饱受心灵创伤的同情。

战争不仅让大量的青春热血丧生，还让死者的亲人因悲伤绝望痛不欲生。战死疆场的士兵留给亲人的是无尽的痛楚与思念。

美国自由诗之父沃尔特·惠特曼的诗歌《爸爸，快从地里回来》描述接到儿子噩耗的一家人的悲苦场面，母亲茶饭不进，只求速死：

虚弱的她披了黑衣
白天，茶饭不进；深夜，不时从噩梦中惊起
惊醒的她啜泣不止
只求无声无息地离开人世
去追随，陪伴她死去的儿子

英国诗人、作曲家艾弗·格尼在《致他的爱人》里这样写道：

他走了，我们所有的计划
都破产了
我们不会再去科茨沃尔德漫步
羊儿静静地在那儿吃草
谁也不理会

和平主义者薇拉·布里坦在《回旋诗》里表达了军人家属万念俱灰的绝望：

你死了，我再无安宁之日
孤自穿梭于寂寥的世界
追梦已是徒劳
因为你死了

英国第一位获得诺贝尔文学奖的作家鲁德亚德·吉卜林一战前是大英帝国狂热的吹鼓手。受他的影响，极富爱国主义情怀的儿子在视力不合格的情形下也渴望参战，建功立业。因为父亲的身份，儿子破格当兵。参战后奔赴法国战场的儿子不久被宣告失踪，焦急万分的吉卜林创作了诗歌《我的儿子杰克》，诗中不断重复的诗行"您可有我儿子杰克的消息？/……/您们有谁听说过他？"深切地表达了老父亲对生不见人，死不见尸的儿子的感情。欧文的战争诗歌《青春挽歌》里这样写道：

> 为他们送终的女孩们脸裹尸布般的苍白
> 坟头的鲜花是满腔的隐忍
> 每一个日暮，他们的亲人都拉上窗帘默哀

在《1916年复活节》，叶芝发出了这悲悯的嗟叹：

> ……
> 太多的牺牲
> 会让心石头般硬
> 什么时候才算够？

（三）犀利地批判现实

著名军事理论家克劳塞维茨曾说："战争是政治的继续，战争的母体是政治。"英国作家乔治·奥威尔说："所有的战争宣传，所有的叫嚣、谎言和仇恨，都来自那些不上战场的人。"

被称为"世界之光""北欧最伟大的人文主义者"的伊拉斯谟在《愚人颂》里说，战争是登峰造极的愚行，它成了一切英雄主

义的源头。什么力量推动德西乌斯们和库尔提乌斯们去自我牺牲？虚荣……

英国诗人、散文家和小说家爱德华·托马斯在其诗歌《这不是简单的对与错》里写道：

这不是政治家或哲学家
能判断的对错
我不讨厌德国人，也不会因为
对英国人的爱而头脑发热
去讨好报纸

亲历战争、战死疆场的欧文用现实主义的笔墨怒斥帝国主义的谎言：

假若你能听见每一次的颠簸
血从肺泡破裂的肺叶中喷出
那肺叶癌细胞一样可怖，喷出的血和恶心的反刍物一样苦
还有无辜的舌头上那不可治愈的溃疡
我的朋友，你就不再会激情洋溢地
向满腔热血的孩子们宣讲
那古老的谎言：为国捐躯
　　　　无上荣光

英年早逝的欧文在诗歌《奇怪的相遇》里这样写道：

"我的朋友,我是你杀死的敌人
我在这黑暗里认出了你
因为昨天你捅我、杀我时,一直眉头紧皱
我躲闪着。但我的手冰冷、无力
现在让我们一起安息……"

在诗歌《这,这就是死亡》里,查尔斯·汉密尔顿·索利断言:

征服者和被征服者在死亡这里无差异:
是懦夫还是勇士,朋友或敌人,鬼魂们不会追问:
"喂,你咽气的时候记录上写的什么?"

吉卜林在奔赴战场的儿子杰克生不见人,死不见尸的情形下亲自到战场上去寻找儿子。当确定唯一的儿子遇难后,绝望的吉卜林开始咒骂战争,咒骂人世。丧子之痛使他一改帝国吹鼓手的口吻,写下了言辞激烈的充满反战情绪的战争墓志铭:

倘若有人问,我们为什么阵亡
告诉他们,只因我们的父辈在说谎

从儿子战友口中得知儿子战死的惨状后,悲伤、内疚的吉卜林曾对妻子说:"需要我跪在你面前来承认是我杀死了我们的儿子吗?"他的《在伦敦遭空袭》的墓志铭这样写道:

在陆地在海洋，我满腹焦虑
我极力逃避征兵，但它弥漫在空气里

从他撰写的墓志铭诗歌《独子》，很容易体味这对老夫妻那白发人送黑发人的悲痛欲绝：

我未杀掉任何人，却要了我母亲的命
她为我伤悲致死（临终还在为她的凶手祈祷）

有些诗谴责战争和发动战争的政客。

现代分析哲学之父霍布斯对人类极度悲观，认为战争是邪恶的，人应渴望、追求和平。被认为是古希腊萨福以来西方最杰出的女诗人艾米莉·狄金森的诗歌《活着似乎是一种耻辱》表达了诗人对战争的必要性的怀疑。这位美国传奇诗人在诗歌中反复追问：为了所谓的自由，巨大的牺牲是否值得？诗人将生命喻为宝贵的珍珠，认为战场是消融珍珠的可怕大碗。

战争诗人西格弗里德·萨松说"战争是祸根"。亲历战争的萨松创作了惊人的现实主义战争诗。《临终时刻》在为死去的年轻士兵悲怜的同时，还犀利地抨击政客：

多点些灯，围在他床边
借给他你的眼、温热的血和活下去的意志
和他说话，唤醒他；也许你能救他
他很年轻，他讨厌战争。当残忍的老竞选者稳操胜券时他怎么能死？

20世纪的伟大诗人W.H.奥登为无名士兵写下这样的墓志铭：

为了拯救你的世界，你让此人去死
如果现在见到你，他可会当面质问你——为什么？

集作家、历史学家、"悖论王子"等诸多身份于一身的G.K.切斯特顿在《乡村庭院中的挽歌》里用犀利的笔墨咒骂决定战事的政客：

为英格兰浴血奋战的人们
却像颗颗流星销匿
为了英格兰
他们在他乡长眠

统治英格兰的人们
在开机密会议
为了英格兰
愿他们死无葬身之地

伊丽莎白·达里尤什写下这样关于战争的诗行：

他们深悉战争魔鬼般闪电的凝视

为屁大的事将他们永远毁灭

1923年荣获诺贝尔文学奖，被艾略特称颂为"我们时代最伟大的诗人"的叶芝在《被请求写一首战争诗》中写道：

这年头，我想
诗人只应沉默
他们哪有能耐给政客正名

多次被提名诺贝尔和平奖的美国诗人大卫·克里格说伊拉克战争是建立在谎言之上的战争，伤害颇广。他认为，这场战争是美国最近一次的十字军东征，它对美国的信誉造成了深刻且无法弥补的损害。我们没有像二战后的纽伦堡审判那样追究那些发起侵略战争的个人罪行。伊拉克人民、儿童都为一场本不应该发生的战争付出了惨痛代价。我们都为一场不必要的、毫无意义的战争付出了沉重的代价，包括那些被派去战斗的美国年轻人，他们在伊拉克作战、牺牲，幸存者带着终身难愈的肉体与心灵的创伤回家。大卫·克里格的诗歌《在巴格达问候布什》鞭挞了发动伊拉克战争的美国总统乔治·布什：

你们的战机毁了我们的家园
接着，你来了
……
你，最不招待见的人

你造成了更多的孤儿寡妻

我将我的左鞋
扔向你一脸的痴笑
右鞋，摔向你满脸的无耻
我唯以此赠你

三、反思战争，珍视和平

战争的幽灵在世界的每一个角落狞笑，自诩为万物之灵长的人类在令人震惊地自相屠戮。《战争：从类人猿到机器人，文明的冲突和演变》一书中对威廉·戈尔丁代表作《蝇王》内容的转述写道："流落在太平洋上、远离学校和规矩的一群男孩懂得了黑暗的事实：人类杀戮成癖，我们的心灵时刻准备着使用暴力。我们就是怪兽，只有一层脆弱的文明加以控制。只要有一丁点的机会，怪兽就会逃脱。"在戈尔丁看来，暴力是存在于基因之中的，是从我们的祖先那里继承来的。文明是唯一的解药，但文明也只能控制其症状，而不能除根。

人类似乎摆脱不了战争，正如英国著名作家、诗人托马斯·哈代的诗行："战争编年史永远继续/只要人类生生不息。"英国传记作家、诗人理查德·奥尔丁顿在《战争叫嚣》里写道："毕竟，总有战争，总有和平/战争总是人群的战争……"究其原因，也许应了战争诗人爱德华·托马斯的诗行："因为太爱自己，我们才仇恨敌人。"

笔者曾在英国剑桥参加了2012年11月11日的阵亡将士纪念日的

纪念活动。仪式上，仅听到一种声音——爱国主义（英雄主义）；听到了弘扬爱国主义诗歌（《佛兰德斯战场》《无名士兵》）的朗诵，还有爱国民歌的合唱，却没有听到任何反思战争、揭露战争残酷的诗篇诵读。事实上，那些反思战争、渴望和平的诗歌更值得我们正视。诗人们在警示我们，为我们提出忠告，只有反思战争，才能珍视和平。

英国史学界大师霍布斯鲍姆回忆，第一次世界大战，从军的牛津与剑桥大学的学生有四分之一阵亡。一战中死去的多是精英阶层。许多英国贵族子弟怀揣《弥尔顿的诗集》走向战场，以展示他们的骑士精神，英国军官死亡率（14.3%）高出普通士兵死亡率（5.8%），大多担任军职的英国贵族死亡率更高达20%。两次世界大战，伊顿公学近2000人为国捐躯（而伊顿公学每年只招收250名学生）。正如意象派运动的发起人庞德的诗行所写"死亡无数/死的都是他们中最优秀的"。

战争不仅剥夺生机勃勃的年轻生命，它带来的心理问题同样是极其恐怖和难以想象的。那些罹患心理疾病的侥幸生还者度日如年，萨松在《令人痛苦的战争经历》里这样写道：

……为什么，你能听到枪声
听。砰，砰，砰——相当柔和……却从未停息——
那些低语的枪声——哦，上帝，我想出去
我要冲他们尖叫，让他们停下来——我要疯了
因为这枪声，我简直、完全要疯了

获得2016年诺贝尔文学奖的鲍勃·迪伦在他早年的歌曲《答案在风中飘扬》中就曾质问："炮弹要多少次掠过天空/才能被永远禁止……一个人有多少只耳朵/才能听见哭声……究竟要失去多少条生命/才能知道太多的人已经死去……"

三次荣获普利策奖、被美国总统林登·约翰逊盛赞为"他就是美国"的卡尔·桑德堡创作了渴望和平的战争诗歌《美国远征军》：

亲爱的，多希望墙上挂着一把生锈的枪
枪的凹槽泛起片片铁锈
一只蜘蛛在它最黑暗、最温暖的角落
织一个银线窝
扳机和测距仪都生锈了
没有手去擦亮，枪就挂在墙上
食指和拇指不经意地指它一下
人们在近乎遗忘或渴望遗忘的情形下会提及这把生锈的枪
冲着蜘蛛说：接着织，很棒

半个多世纪前的甲壳虫乐队的影响力依然强劲。列侬的《想象》至今感染、震撼着全世界的听众：

想象这世上的人们，都享受着当下……

想象没有国家
这不费什么力气

不去消灭谁，也不为谁就义
也没有宗教分歧
所有的人们，都生活在和平里……
……
四海皆兄弟
所有的人们，一同享受这世界的美丽……

正如越南战争时期伟大的反战歌曲——《战争》里的呐喊："战争有何益处，一无是处。它只会吞噬无辜的生命……"

反思战争的目的是希望"给和平一个机会"。约翰·列侬的歌《给和平一个机会》迄今依然值得我们颂唱和反思。

人人都在谈论
套袋主义，杂乱主义，拖沓主义，癫狂主义，邋遢主义，肮脏主义
这主义，那主义，主义主义主义？

我们只想说 给和平一个机会
我们只想说 给和平一个机会

马太·保罗·米勒的英文歌曲《终有一天》（*One Day*）能火遍全球，正说明善良的人们都期盼和平，期盼人类安然相处：

这是我一生的期待
是我一直的祈祷

人们终能说

不想再打仗了

再也没有战争了

我们的孩子们能开心玩耍

终有一天

不再是什么

赢或输

　　人类必须消灭战争，否则战争将消灭人类。美国著名的人类学家玛格丽特·米德认为："战争不过是一种发明。"令人感到鼓舞的是她和许多研究者都认为"糟糕的发明总会被更好的发明所取代。"他们证明了人类的自然状态是和平的。

　　愿世上的人们能安然相处，愿我们未来的世界如英国诗人A.E.豪斯曼在《战争归来的士兵》中的诗行所描写的那样：

战争结束了，和平了

欢迎你，欢迎所有人

战马收割三叶草时

他的缰绳挂在马厩里

终于无须在冰天雪地里煎熬了

不用从秋到春在壕沟里与污秽同住

也无须在汗喷喷的夏天

为恺撒或国王打仗

歇歇吧，战马；生锈吧，马笼头
国王们，恺撒们，留着你们的薪酬
士兵，愿你能在夜晚的酒吧
永远地坐下来，放松

诗人或者诗歌都无法阻止战争，但可以让我们反思战争，反思的目的是为了"给和平一个机会"，唯愿世界和平！

目录

罗伯特·骚塞

布连海姆战役后 / 003

阿尔弗雷德·丁尼生

轻骑兵冲锋 / 009

沃尔特·惠特曼

敲啊！敲啊！战鼓！/ 015　　爸爸，快从地里回来 / 017

最英勇的士兵 / 020

艾米莉·狄金森

活着似乎是一种耻辱 / 022

托马斯·哈代

他杀掉的那个人 / 026　　年轻的鼓手霍奇 / 028　　国破之际 / 030

罗伯特·路易斯·史蒂文森

安魂曲 / 033

A. E. 豪斯曼

雇佣兵的墓志铭 / 036　　　我们在此长眠 / 037

致英年早逝的运动员（节选）/ 038　　战争归来的士兵 / 040

凯瑟琳·泰南

参军 / 043

威廉·巴特勒·叶芝

被请求写首战争诗 / 046　　1916年复活节（节选）/ 047

一个爱尔兰飞行员预见了死亡 / 048

约瑟夫·鲁德亚德·吉卜林

两个加拿大纪念馆 / 051　　我的儿子杰克 / 052　　常态 / 054

无名女尸 / 055　　萨洛尼卡墓地 / 056　　独子 / 057

在伦敦遭空袭 / 058

罗伯特·劳伦斯·比扬

献给阵亡将士 / 061

夏洛特·玛丽·缪

无名战士纪念碑 / 064

约翰·麦克雷

在佛兰德斯战场 / 067

沃尔特·德·拉·梅尔

拿破仑 / 070

罗伯特·塞维斯

双胞胎 / 073

G. K. 切斯特顿

乡村庭院中的挽歌 / 076

卡尔·桑德堡

美国远征军 / 079　　　草 / 080　　　他们照令执行 / 082

菲利普·爱德华·托马斯

号角 / 085　　　这不是简单的对与错 / 087

威尔弗里德·威尔逊·吉布森

早餐 / 090　　　信息 / 091

华莱士·史蒂文斯

阶段性 / 094

萨拉·蒂斯代尔

战时的春天 / 098

埃兹拉·庞德

休·塞尔温·毛伯利（节选）/ 101

西格弗里德·萨松

要紧吗？/ 107　　　无用的司令部军官 / 108
于我体内，过去、现在、将来会集 / 109　　　致所有阵亡的军官 / 110

临终时刻/ 113　　令人痛苦的战争经历/ 116　　宽恕/ 118
梦想家/ 119　　"他们"/ 120　　在战壕里自杀/ 121

鲁伯特·布鲁克
士兵/ 124　　逝者/ 125

伊丽莎白·达里尤什
献给美索不达米亚战役的幸存者/ 127

艾伦·西格
我和死亡有个约会/ 130

艾弗·格尼
致他的爱人/ 134

艾萨克·罗森伯格
运兵船/ 137

理查德·奥尔丁顿
战争叫嚣/ 140　　战壕诗/ 146

威尔弗雷德·欧文
奇怪的相遇/ 150　　无效/ 153　　自残/ 154
为国捐躯/ 157　　青春挽歌/ 159

玛格丽特·伊莎贝尔·科尔夫人
落叶/ 161　　老兵/ 162

多萝西·帕克

老兵 / 165

梅·韦德伯恩·坎南

1914年8月 / 167　　战后 / 169

薇拉·布里坦

也许 / 172　　回旋诗 / 174　　1914年8月 / 175

查尔斯·汉密尔顿·索利

这，这就是死亡 / 178　　当你看到数百万无嘴的死人 / 179

罗伯特·格雷夫斯

死去的波奇 / 182

塞西尔·戴·刘易斯

志愿军 / 185

约翰·贝杰曼

泥沼 / 188　　在威斯敏斯特教堂 / 191

W. H. 奥登

无名士兵墓志铭 / 196　　阿喀琉斯之盾 / 197

克利福德·戴门特

儿子 / 203

狄兰·托马斯
那只签署文件的手 / 206

伊芙·梅里亚姆
懦夫 / 208

约翰·列侬
想象 / 211　　　　　　　　给和平一个机会 / 213

大卫·克里格
伊拉克孩子有姓名 / 218　　　　比战争更糟糕的 / 221
致一名伊拉克男孩——阿里·伊斯梅尔·阿巴斯 / 223
在巴格达问候布什 / 225　　　　扎伊德的不幸 / 227

安德鲁·莫伸
哈里·帕奇之死 / 231　　　　　政权更迭 / 233

附录 / 235

译后记 / 356

罗伯特·骚塞（Robert Southey，1774—1843）

英国桂冠诗人。他将许多词汇引入英语。他的《布连海姆战役后》是最早的反战诗之一。

浪漫主义诗人，作家。与威廉·华兹华斯和塞缪尔·柯勒律治一同被称为"湖畔诗人"。因才华横溢被柯勒律治称为"文学上的通才"。

生于英国布里斯托尔的商人之家。曾在威斯敏斯特学校就读，因撰写了一篇反对学校体罚学生的文章被开除学籍。之后来到牛津大学贝利奥尔学院学习。在校期间，因沉醉于法国大革命，撰写长诗《圣女贞德》（*Joan of Arc*）。之后结识诗人柯勒律治，二人合著剧本《罗伯斯庇尔的堕落》（*The Fall of Robespierre*）。1808年，写下《来自英格兰的信》（*Letters from England*）。1809至1838年一直为期刊《季度评论》撰文。1813年获得"桂冠诗人"头衔。1819年认识了苏格兰土木工程师托马斯·特尔福德，并随其到苏格兰高地考察工程项目，1829年发表作品《1819年苏格兰旅行日记》（*Journal of a Tour in Scotland in 1819*）。1837年收到夏洛蒂·勃朗特的一封来信，信中夏洛蒂希望能得到他的指点，骚塞盛赞她的创作天赋，但同时写道："文学不应该是女人的事业。"骚塞将许多词汇引入英语,譬如,"自传"(autobiography)一词。他撰写了不少名人传记,譬如约翰·班扬、约翰·卫斯理、威廉·考珀、奥立佛·克伦威尔、霍雷肖·纳尔逊等。出版过童话故事《三只小熊》(*The Story of the Three Bears*)。他的名诗《布连海姆战役后》(*After Blenheim*)是最早的反战诗篇之一。骚塞还是著名的葡萄牙语和西班牙语学者,翻译了不少作品。此外,他还撰写了一些历史书籍,如《巴西历史》(*History of Brazil*)和《半岛战争史》(*History of the Peninsular War*)等。

晚年的他因思想趋于保守而招致同时代的文人诸如拜伦等的不齿。逝后葬于克罗斯威特教堂。

布连海姆战役①后

一个夏天的傍晚,
老卡斯帕尔把农活做完,
在夕阳的余晖里,
静坐在屋前。
小孙女威勒玛茵,
在一旁的草地上嬉戏。
看到哥哥皮特金,
滚动着一个东西又大又圆,
那是他玩耍时捡来的,
在一个小河边。
皮特金请教爷爷,
这又大又光又圆的东西是啥。
老人端在手里,
孩子们一旁站立,满脸好奇。
老人摇摇头,
一声叹息:
 "这是一个可怜士兵的骷髅,
他死于那场伟大的战役。"
 "我在菜园里也发现过,
这周围到处都是。
耕地时,
犁头常从土中翻起。

曾有几千名战士,
死于那场伟大的胜利。"
　　"给我们讲讲事件的究竟吧,"
小皮特金迫不及待,
威勒玛茵也仰起小脸,
睁大眼睛,满眼惊疑。
　　"究竟为什么
打那场战役?"
　　"那场战役,英国人
把法国人打得溃不成军。
但究竟为了什么,
我也说不清道不明。
但人们都说,"老人附和着,
　　"那场战役赫赫有名。"
　　"我父亲那时就住在布连海姆,
距那条河不远的地方;
他们一把火烧毁他的房,
父亲被迫背井离乡:
携家小四处流浪,
只为寻一个安身的地方。"
　　"战火毁了一切,
方圆多少里一片荒凉;
多少母亲和孩子,
在战火中悲惨死去。

你们可知,每场著名战役后,
都是满目疮痍。"
"据说我们虽赢得胜利,
但战后景象却令人神伤,
遍地的尸体,
在烈日下腐烂。
你们可知,每次大胜仗后,
都是这番惨状。"
"马尔勃罗公爵②获得最高嘉奖,
尤金亲王③也无上荣光。"
"但这多么残忍啊!"
小威勒玛茵打断了他,
"哎……哎……我的小孙女,
那可是举世瞩目的胜利。"
"人人都对公爵倍加赞誉,
是他赢得了这伟大的胜利。"
"可究竟有什么裨益呢?"
小皮特金学着大人的口气,
"这我也说不清,道不明,"老人喃喃自语,
"但那可是举世瞩目的胜利。"④

注释

① 指西班牙王位继承战争(1701—1714)中的一次战役。奥地利、英国、荷兰联军与法国-巴伐利亚联军于1704年8月13日

在巴伐利亚的布连海姆村附近的决定性交战。英国的马尔勃罗公爵和奥地利的尤金亲王联合击破了法国-巴伐利亚联军。这一胜利决定了法国的败局。

② 马尔勃罗公爵：约翰·丘吉尔（1650—1722），英国政治家、军事家。英国首相温斯顿·丘吉尔和戴安娜王妃都是他的后裔。

③ 尤金亲王（1663—1736）：欧洲著名军事统帅。曾经服务于哈布斯堡的三朝皇帝。

④ 该诗通过孩童的好奇揭示战争的暴行，即人类之间互相残杀的劣行。

阿尔弗雷德·丁尼生（Alfred Tennyson，1809—1892）

任职最久的桂冠诗人。T.S.艾略特称之为"英伦最伤感的诗人。"他诗歌里的许多词语已成为英语的常态表达。

继华兹华斯之后的英国桂冠诗人。怀特岛上的丁尼生山和丁尼生小径都以他的名字命名，山顶上矗立着他的纪念碑。

出生于牧师家庭，12个孩子中排行第四位。作为牧师的父亲非常注重孩子的教育，丁尼生和兄弟们从小就热爱读书和写作。后进入剑桥三一学院学习。同年，丁尼生和哥哥查尔斯出版诗集《两兄弟诗集》（*Poems by Two Brothers*）。剑桥求学期间，才华横溢的室友亚瑟·海拉姆——一位史学家的儿子，对丁尼生的诗歌创作给予了最初也是最重要的支持和鼓励。1830年和1832年，他们两次周游欧洲。1830年丁尼生因诗歌《廷巴克图》（*Timbuktu*）获得剑桥大学的"校长金牌"奖。同年出版自己的诗集《抒情诗》（*Poems，Chiefly Lyrical*），他最著名的诗歌《克拉利贝尔》（*Claribel*）和《玛丽安娜》（*Mariana*）等出自本诗集。其早期诗歌对拉斐尔前派兄弟会产生了重大影响。1831年，父亲去世，丁尼生不得不回家照料家事，未获得学位。1832年，好友海拉姆（已成为丁尼生妹妹的未婚夫）的突然离世使丁尼生无限悲伤。此后，

10年间未发表作品。1842年,在朋友的劝说下,出版两卷《诗集》(*Poems*),第一卷是对已出版诗歌的总结,第二卷是新诗,包括代表诗歌《洛克斯利大厅》(*Locksley Hall*)、《冲啊,冲啊,冲啊》(*Break, Break, Break*)以及《尤利西斯》(*Ulysses*)。5年后,丁尼生又发表了长篇叙事诗《公主》(*The Princess*),试图证明女人最大的成就是幸福的婚姻。1850年,出版挽诗《悼念》(*In Memoriam*),该作品是英国文学中最伟大的挽歌之一,他也因此成为最受欢迎的诗人之一。同年,因为塞缪尔·罗格斯的婉拒,丁尼生获得了继华兹华斯之后的"桂冠诗人"头衔。1855年出版又一代表作《轻骑兵冲锋》(*The Charge of the Light Brigade*)。该诗讴歌英国骑兵在克里米亚战争巴拉克拉瓦战役中的英雄气概。1859年出版的诗歌《国王之歌》(*Idylls of the Kings*)热销。1884年,被授予贵族爵位。1892年去世,葬于威斯敏斯特大教堂。

他诗歌里的许多词语已成为英语的常态表达。当时舆论认为,在世的诗人中无一人有资格继他之后成为新的桂冠诗人。为了表示敬意,桂冠诗人一职在他去世后空缺了4年。T.S.艾略特称他为"英伦最伤感的诗人"。

轻骑兵冲锋[1]

半里格[2],半里格
往前冲杀半里格
骑兵六百名
挺进死亡谷
只听"向前冲,轻骑兵!
向炮火冲锋!"
骑兵六百名
冲进死亡谷

"向前冲,轻骑兵!"
可有人惊慌沮丧?
没有。尽管他们心知肚明
这是错误的命令
但他们无权反映
他们不能质疑
只能奉命去牺牲
冲进死亡谷
骑兵六百名

炮打在他们右面
炮打在他们左面
炮打在他们前面

炮火轰鸣

他们善骑又果敢

冒着炮火和霰弹

骑兵六百名

冲进地狱门

拥抱死神

出鞘军刀明晃晃

空中挥舞闪寒光

劈向敌军炮手身上

英勇轻骑兵

举世震惊

杀进炮火硝烟

直冲防线

哥萨克人和俄国人

挡不住劈来的军刀

乱了队形

遭遇英勇的骑兵六百名

只能认怂

炮打在他们右面

炮打在他们左面

炮打在他们后面

炮火轰鸣

冒着炮火和霰弹

他们勇猛作战

有战马和英雄倒下

他们中生还的勇士们

冲出死神的魔爪

六百人中生还的勇士们

冲出地狱门

时间怎能湮没英名？

这次勇敢的进攻

举世震惊

致敬，向这次冲锋！

致敬，向这六百名

豪迈轻骑兵！

注释

① 《轻骑兵冲锋》是为讴歌英国骑兵在克里米亚战争巴拉克拉瓦战役中表现出的英雄气概。诗作在这次战役的六周后出版。因错误的指挥，由卡迪根勋爵率领的仅装备马刀的英国轻骑兵在易守难攻的地形上，正面冲向准备充足的俄军炮兵。勇敢的轻骑旅在猛烈的炮火下，成功冲入炮兵阵地，但因伤亡惨重，被迫撤退。付出了沉重代价的英军没有实际受益。该诗字里行间中歌颂轻骑兵英勇牺牲的崇高精神，诗作亦成为这场冲锋被后人铭记的原因。

② 里格（league）：是古老的陆地及海洋的长度测量单位。在陆地上，1里格通常被认为是3英里，即4.827千米。在海洋中，1里格通常被认为是3海里，即5.556千米。此测量单位已不再被官方使用。

沃尔特·惠特曼（Walt Whitman，1819—1892）

惠特曼是美国文坛中最有影响力的诗人之一，常被称为自由诗之父。评论家哈罗德·布鲁姆称其是美国想象力之父。

  美国诗人、散文家和记者，美国文坛中最有影响力的诗人之一，常被称为自由诗之父。

  生于纽约长岛。父亲是农夫兼木匠，无法保证其良好的教育。11岁时，离开学校挣钱糊口，先后当过学徒、排字工、记者、教师和政府职员。1855年自费出版《草叶集》（Leaves of Grass），试图让普通人接触美国史诗。他在林肯去世时写下了著名的诗篇《啊，船长！我的船长！》（O Captain! My Captain!）和《当紫丁香最后一次在庭院绽放》（When Lilacs Last in the Dooryard Bloom'd），并做了一系列的演讲。晚年中风后，搬到了新泽西州的卡姆登。72岁辞世，葬礼以公开的方式进行。

  惠特曼身处超验主义和现实主义的变革时期，其作品对美国诗歌产生了深远的影响。"垮掉派"的核心人物金斯堡奉其为自己的精神父亲。玛丽·史密斯·惠特尔·科斯特洛认为："没有沃尔特·惠特曼，就没有《草叶集》，你则无法真正理解美国。"现代主义诗人埃兹拉·庞德称惠特曼为"美国的诗人……。他就是美国"。博尔赫斯以一首十四行诗向他致敬。

敲啊！敲啊！战鼓！

敲啊！敲啊！战鼓！——吹啊！吹啊！军号！
穿过窗——穿过门——像暴徒一样
冲进庄严的教堂，驱散会众
冲进学生正在学习的学堂
新郎不得安静——不能和新娘享受爱情
农夫不得安宁，不能收割、耕种
鼓，你就这样狂暴地擂——号，你就这样尖厉地吹

敲啊！敲啊！战鼓！——吹啊！吹啊！军号！
淹没城市的噪声——淹没车轮的隆隆轰鸣
买方卖方难以讨价还价——掮客投机商束手无策——他们
　　岂能继续？
演讲者怎能演讲？歌手怎能高歌？
律师怎能在法庭向法官陈述案情？
夜深了，却无人能眠
鼓，你就更急更重地擂——号，你就更猛更野地吹！

敲啊！敲啊！战鼓！——吹啊！吹啊！军号！
无需停歇——无需听从规劝
无需理会那些胆小鬼——那些哭泣的和祈祷的
无需在意恳请年轻人的老翁
淹没孩童们的哭闹声，无需理会妈妈们的恳请

把灵床上等待入殓的死人们也震醒
啊,可怕的鼓,你就这样重重地擂——号,你就这样刺耳
　　地吹!

爸爸，快从地里回来

爸爸，快从地里回来，皮特来信了
妈妈，快到前门来，这有您儿子的信

瞧，正值深秋
树木更绿，更红，更黄
树叶在微风中摇曳，俄亥俄州①的村庄恬静、清爽
果园的苹果熟了，葡萄藤上缀着串串葡萄
（你可闻到藤蔓上葡萄的酸甜？
可嗅到嗡嗡的蜜蜂忙碌其间的荞麦的芳香？）

看，雨后的天空明亮、恬静，白云朵朵
蓝天下，整个农场繁茂葱郁，万物祥和，生机勃勃

田野草木葳蕤
听到女儿的召唤，父亲莫名地有点慌乱
母亲也立刻走向门前

她急匆匆地，不祥的预感使她步履蹒跚
来不及梳凌乱的头发，顾不上扶正帽子

她急忙撕开信封
啊，信不是儿子写的，却有儿子的署名

啊，亲儿子的信竟是陌生的笔迹，母亲顿感晴天霹雳！
只觉地转天旋，眼前发黑，仅捕捉到只语片言
"遭骑兵突袭，胸口中弹，被送往医院
体虚，不久会好转。"
城乡交融的俄亥俄，熙熙攘攘
一派繁华景象
此时的她，脸色苍白，倚着门框
虚弱异常

"亲爱的妈妈，您不要太难过，"（刚成年的女儿啜泣
　　着，小姐妹们神情沮丧，无言地簇拥身旁）
"妈妈，信中说皮特很快就康复。"

哎，可怜的孩子，他怎会康复，（那个勇敢、纯洁的灵魂，
　　再无机会康复）
他们捎来信时，他已经死了
她唯一的儿子已经死了

肝肠寸断的母亲仍须打起精神
虚弱的她披了黑衣
白天，茶饭不进；深夜，不时从噩梦中惊起
惊醒的她啜泣不止
只求无声无息地离开人世
去追随，陪伴她死去的儿子

注释

① 俄亥俄州：美国中西部的一个州，因属地内的俄亥俄河得名。"俄亥俄"印第安语是"大河"的意思，俄亥俄河是密西西比河最大的支流。州政府位于哥伦布市。

最英勇的士兵

从战场上生还的士兵被冠以盛名——英勇
那勇敢地冲在前方、阵亡的士兵，籍籍无名

艾米莉·狄金森（Emily Dickinson，1830—1886）

被认为是古希腊萨福以来西方最杰出的女诗人。

美国传奇女诗人。与惠特曼齐名。1994年被评论家列为西方文明的26位核心作家之一。

出生在马萨诸塞州阿默斯特的一个显赫家庭。年轻时，在阿默斯特学院学习了7年，后短暂地就读于芒特·霍利约克女子神学院。25岁开始弃绝社交，大部分时间过着与世隔绝的生活。终身未婚。与朋友之间的交流主要通过信函。文学史上称她为"阿默斯特的女尼"。

虽然是一位多产的作家，但生前仅发表了10首诗及一封信。身后随着她的诗歌为世人所知，声名剧增。她的诗独一无二，通常没有标题，经常使用斜韵以及非常规的大写字母和标点符号，特别是破折号。其诗行简短，诗作多涉及死亡、永生、美学、爱情、自然和精神等主题。其诗风凝练，意象清新，描绘细微，思想深邃，被视为20世纪现代主义诗歌的先驱之一。代表作有《希望》（*Hope*）《我是无名之辈！》（*I'm Nobody！*）、《我从未见过的荒原》（*I Never Saw a Moor*）、《因为我不能停步等待死神》（*Because I Could not Stop for Death*）等。

富有创新意识的她如今被认为是美国文化里的一个不朽的人物。

活着似乎是一种耻辱[1]

活着似乎是一种耻辱——
当勇敢的人们——死去
人们羡慕——因接纳了他们头颅——
而卓绝的泥土——

石碑讲述着——逝去的勇士
是为了保卫谁
他们的一丝一毫——我们难以具备
他们为我们的自由付费——

高昂的代价——昂贵地支付
我们能否承受——
那钱垛一样多的尸体——
换得的所有?

静待胜利的我们可值得
那么多珍珠般的生命——
为我们——牺牲——
在战争的大碗里消融?

活着——兴许是一种殊荣——
想着那些死去的人们——

无名的神灵

在彰显神性

注释

① 这首诗的背景是美国南北战争。该诗是艾米莉作为幸存者赠给弗雷泽·斯特恩斯的内疚之诗。诗歌有反战意味，诗人怀疑战争的必要性，反复追问：为了所谓的自由，巨大的牺牲是否值得？她将生命喻为宝贵的珍珠，认为战场是消融珍珠的可怕大碗。

托马斯·哈代（Thomas Hardy, 1840—1928）

英国19世纪后期最重要的小说家、诗人之一。对英国文学影响深远。

  英国著名小说家和诗人。作为19世纪后期的一位文学大师，他用艺术的手法概述了这一时期英国乡村的风土人情和社会面貌，促使英国的现实主义创作再度繁荣。

  1840年生于英国多塞特郡的上博克汉普顿，小学教育一直持续到16岁，之后他被送到当地建筑师约翰·希克斯那里当学徒。曾梦想上大学及成为一名圣公会牧师，但由于经济困难加之对宗教缺乏兴趣，开始尝试写作。17岁时第一部小说手稿《穷人和女人》（*The Poor Man and the Lady*）被数家出版商拒绝，但编辑乔治·梅雷迪斯鼓励他不要放弃。1871年《非常手段》（*Desperate Remedies*）成功出版。1872年出版的《绿荫下》（*Under the Greenwood Tree*）完美地展示了其写作风格。1874年与艾玛·拉维尼娅·吉福德喜结连理。在艾玛的鼓励下，投入到文学事业中。

  他的小说《远离尘嚣》（*Far From the Madding Crowd*）、《还乡》（*The Return of the Native*）、《卡斯特桥市长》（*The Mayor of Casterbridge*）、《德伯家的苔丝》（*Tess of the d'Urbervilles*）和《无

名的裘德》（*Jude the Obscure*）等多以威塞克斯地区为背景。1896年，他又重新转向诗歌创作。余生一直在写短篇小说、诗歌和戏剧。有两卷诗集（大约900首诗歌）和短篇小说问世。其诗歌为英国诗歌从文雅的乔治亚时代诗风转向现代诗风的过程中起到承上启下的作用。1912年，妻子艾玛去世。1914年与弗洛伦斯·艾米丽·杜格代尔结婚。死后被埋葬在威斯敏斯特教堂的诗人角，他的心脏则被葬在家乡的圣米迦勒教堂墓地，陪伴他的先辈和两任妻子。

他的诗歌极大地影响了美国诗人罗伯特·弗罗斯特、W.H.奥登、菲利普·拉金等。此外，针对当时的布尔战争、第一次世界大战，哈代创作了一些著名的战争诗歌，他的战争诗歌深深地影响了战争诗人鲁伯特·布鲁克和萨松。弗吉尼亚·伍尔夫认为，哈代具有世界视角，他关注人类的命运。

他杀掉的那个人[①]

倘若我们在某个老字号餐馆
相遇
我们会坐下来
举杯畅饮

但此刻我们都是步兵
我们怒目相向
我射向他,他射向我
最后我把他杀死在他的阵地上

我射死他因为——
他是我的敌人
是的,他就是我的敌人
千真万确

也许他知道自己入伍
只是临时的——就像我——
因为失业——无事可做
不为别的

战争的确古怪离奇
使你向另一个人射击

倘若酒吧相遇

你会与他举杯畅饮

注释

① 此诗写于1902年。大多数英国人都支持布尔战争，哈代逆向而行，反战。布尔（Boer）一词源于荷兰语，意为农民。布尔战争是英国在南非与荷兰、法国、德国等白人移民的后代布尔人之间的战争。布尔战争共有两次。第一次布尔战争（1880.12—1881.3）是英国人与布尔人之间的小规模战争，获胜的布尔人被英国授予了自治权。第二次布尔战争（1899—1902）是英国为了争夺南非当地丰富的金矿而挑起的战争。通常说的布尔战争指第二次布尔战争。

年轻的鼓手霍奇[①]

他们把鼓手霍奇抛进坑里,让他安息
没有棺木的他——和他们发现他时一样
那座耸立在草原的小山
是他的纪念碑
异乡的星辰美丽璀璨
每夜在他坟冢上闪现

他刚从故乡威塞克斯[②]来
不晓得广阔的非洲高原
意味着什么
不了解莽莽丛林和尘埃飞扬的沃土
更不知奇异的星
缘何在茫茫暮霭中升到天空

这草原的一隅
是霍奇的安息地
他北方人那厚实的胸膛和蕴含朴实思想的头颅
将长成一棵南国大树
那异域的星光
永远闪烁在他坟上

注释

① 本诗写于1902年,为在布尔战争中战死的英国士兵而作。这首诗对歌颂战争加以批判。

② 威塞克斯(Wessex):哈代家乡,英国的多塞特郡的古地名。

国破之际

仅一人在犁地
踽踽在广袤的田野里
一匹老马踉跄前行
半睡半醒

一缕炊烟从茅草堆
袅袅升起
同样的故事仍会继续
纵使朝代更易

远处走来一对情侣
窃窃私语
战争编年史永远继续
只要人类生生不息

罗伯特·路易斯·史蒂文森
（Robert Louis Stevenson，1850—1894）

作品在全球被广泛翻译。影响力仅次于查尔斯·狄更斯。

苏格兰小说家、散文家、诗人和旅行作家。代表作有《金银岛》（*Treasure Island*）、《化身博士》（*Strange Case of Dr Jekyll and Mr Hyde*）、《绑架》（*Kidnapped*）和《儿童诗歌花园》（*A Child's Garden of Verses*）等。

出生于爱丁堡，家中独子，父亲是位灯塔工程师。从小体弱，患有严重的支气管疾病，经常无法上学，长期由私人教师辅导。读书很晚，但他时常向母亲和护士口述故事，他的父亲为他这种兴趣感到自豪。16岁出资印刷了他的第一本出版物《彭特兰起义：历史的一页，1666年》。17岁时，进入爱丁堡大学攻读工程学，后转学法律，但他并未从事律师行业，却专职写作。1883年出版《金银岛》，第一次尝到真正的成功。同年史蒂文森最著名的小说《化身博士》也在出版6个月内售出4万册，奠定了其文学声誉，他成为英国文学的领军人物之一。肺结核一直困扰着他。虽然体弱，但他仍大量写作并经常旅行。1888年，在医生的建议下，考虑搬到气候温暖的地方，于是与家人启航前往南太平洋。1890年，定居萨摩亚。

在那里，他的写作从浪漫和冒险小说转向了现实主义。1894年，在岛上的家中去世，享年44岁。

安魂曲[①]

辽阔的天空,璀璨星光
挖个坟墓,把死去的我埋葬
我快乐地活,欣慰地亡
唯有一个小愿望

请在我的墓碑上刻下这诗行
"就像水手的家是海洋
猎人的家在山岗
这里的他躺在他渴望的地方"

注释

[①] 该诗被刻在作者的墓碑上,还被电影《菲律宾浴血战》引用,表达为国浴血奋战的将士视死如归的气概。

A.E.豪斯曼

（Alfred Edward Housman，1859—1936）

最优秀的学者之一。

英国诗人、学者。生于英格兰伍斯特郡的福克伯里，7个孩子中的老大。1877年，进入牛津大学圣约翰学院学习，在古典文学考试中成绩最佳。但当他爱上了室友摩西·杰克逊后，期末成绩竟不及格，他设法通过了最后一年的考试。后来在伦敦专利局当了10年职员。期间，深入学习希腊和罗马古典文学，1892年被任命为伦敦大学的拉丁语教授。1911年，成为剑桥大学三一学院的拉丁语教授，直至去世。

一生只出版了两本诗集：《什罗普郡少年》（*A Shropshire Lad*）和《最后的诗》（*Last Poems*）。《什罗普郡少年》围绕田园之美、单恋、短暂的青春、悲伤、死亡和普通士兵的爱国主义等主题展开。因手稿遭到多家出版商的拒绝，后自费出版，这让同事和学生们颇为惊讶。战争让《什罗普郡少年》颇受关注，一些作曲家为作品谱曲，提升了作品的知名度。

20世纪20年代初，当老室友摩西·杰克逊生命垂危时，为了心仪的恋人，豪斯曼将最好的未发表的诗歌汇编成《最后的诗歌》

出版，大获成功。他被誉为最优秀的学者之一，但拒绝荣誉，过着隐居生活，后在剑桥去世。他的第三部作品《更多的诗歌》(*More Poems*)在他逝后由其兄弟劳伦斯出版。

雇佣兵的墓志铭

天塌
地陷
雇佣兵们听从召唤
他们领了薪酬,继而阵亡

他们的肩膀支撑着欲倾的天
他们挺立着,地才没有下陷
上帝抛弃的,他们保卫
还省了一大笔钱

我们在此长眠

我们在此长眠
我们别无选择
要活就会使生养我们的祖国
蒙羞

毋庸置疑
生命没有太多可以挥霍
年轻人认为可以
我们也曾年轻过

致英年早逝的运动员[①]（节选）

当年，你为小镇赢得比赛
我们擎起你，穿过市场
男女老少夹道为你鼓掌
荣归故里的你被举在肩上

今天，人们又聚集路上
抬你在肩上
轻轻放你于坟墓
小镇格外肃穆

英明的你提早离去
赛场的桂冠不会永远属于你
月桂[②]苍翠
但它的凋败远超玫瑰

闭上双眼的你
看不到记录被打破
长眠于地下的你
兴许更享受这沉寂

注释

① 该诗发表于两次布尔战争之间,在第一次世界大战期间(众多年轻人血洒疆场)广为传颂。该诗被电影《走出非洲》引用。

② 月桂:根据希腊神话,指四季常青的植物。这里指冠军头衔。

战争归来的士兵

战场归来的士兵
被占领城镇的破坏者
这儿有不花钱的安逸
来,坐下歇息

战争结束了,和平了
欢迎你,欢迎所有人
战马收割三叶草时
他的缰绳挂在马厩里

终于无须在冰天雪地里煎熬了
不用从秋到春在壕沟里与污秽同住
也无须在汗喷喷的夏天
为恺撒①或国王打仗

歇歇吧,战马;生锈吧,马笼头
国王们,恺撒们,留着你们的薪酬
士兵,愿你能在夜晚的酒吧
永远地坐下来,放松

注释

① 恺撒：源于罗马帝国杰出的军事统帅、政治家尤里乌斯·恺撒大帝的姓氏，后成为帝王、皇帝的头衔（称谓）。德语中的皇帝（kaiser）与俄语中的沙皇（tsar）均源于此。

凯瑟琳·泰南（Katharine Tynan，1859/1861—1931）

为爱尔兰的文学复兴作出了巨大的贡献。诗人叶芝受到了她的影响和启发。

爱尔兰女作家、记者，以小说和诗歌闻名。生于都柏林郡的一个小农家庭，在德罗赫达的圣凯瑟琳修道院接受教育。她的第一首诗歌《梦》（*Dream*）发表于1878年。20多岁的她已是都柏林文学圈里的中心人物。叶芝仰慕她的才华，说受到了她的影响和启发。

她一生创作了100多部小说，12部短篇小说集、回忆录、剧本和十几本诗集，为爱尔兰文学复兴作出了巨大的贡献。其作品关注女权运动、爱尔兰民族事业等。代表作包括《路易丝·德拉·瓦利埃和其他诗歌》（*Louise de la Vallière and Other Poems*）、《三叶草》（*Shamrock*s）、《歌谣和抒情诗》（*Ballads and Lyrics*）、《爱尔兰诗歌》（*Irish Poems*）等。

参　军

他们步履矫健，步伐整齐
他们，面颊圆润，金发灿灿，却将成为炮灰
他们满面欢喜，仿佛去参加婚礼
可怜的孩子们

昏暗的街道凝望着他们，一排又一排
在奔驰的电车上，无忧无虑的他们云雀般歌唱
他们英勇无惧，坚定前行
歌唱着走进黑暗

和着锡哨、口琴声
他们歌唱着，走向荣耀坟墓
无知的、快乐的金发男孩们
爱也无能为力

可敬的勇气！崇高的精神！被他们吻过的可怜女孩们
快快和他们一起奔跑吧：他们再吻不到你们了
他们歌唱着
从青春的混沌走向生命的终极

威廉·巴特勒·叶芝（William Butler Yeats，1865—1939）

1923年荣获诺贝尔文学奖，庞德说他是"唯一值得认真研究的诗人"。艾略特称颂他为"我们时代最伟大的诗人"。

爱尔兰诗人、戏剧家、散文家、画家。爱尔兰文艺复兴的中心人物，20世纪西方最有成就的诗人之一。对当代英国与爱尔兰诗歌的发展影响巨大，被艾略特称颂为"我们时代最伟大的诗人"。

生于爱尔兰都柏林的艺术世家，早年大部分时间在伦敦度过，17岁时开始诗歌创作。1884年至1886年期间，在托马斯街的大都会艺术学院（现国立艺术与设计学院）就读。1885年在《都柏林大学评论》发表诗作。他的第一本个人出版物《摩沙达：戏剧化的诗》（*Mosada：A Dramatic Poem*）由父亲出资印刷了100本。早期作品大量借鉴了雪莱、埃德蒙·斯宾塞以及拉斐尔前派诗歌的修辞和色彩。随后出版的诗集《奥辛的漫游和其他诗歌》（*The Wanderings of Oisin and Other Poems*）收录了一系列可以追溯到19世纪80年代中期的诗歌。

其戏剧颇受奥斯卡·王尔德的影响。1891年，叶芝出版了《约翰·谢尔曼》（*John Sherman*）和《多亚》（*Dhoya*）。叶芝一生都对神秘主义、招魂术和占星术感兴趣，广泛阅读这些主题的作品，是超自然研究组织"幽灵俱乐部"的成员。1909年，庞德去伦敦的部分原因是为了拜见他，庞德认为他是"唯一值得认真研究的诗人"。1916年，庞德以秘书的身份为他工作，协调《诗歌》杂志发表叶芝的诗作。叶芝一生颇富戏剧性。对茅德·岗长达几十年的追求未果。1917年，向25岁的乔治·海德·李斯求婚，婚后孕育了两个孩子。

1923年12月，以"他充满灵感的诗歌总是以高度艺术的形式表达了整个民族的精神"获得了诺贝尔文学奖。后期的重要作品有《库尔的野天鹅》（*The Wild Swans at Coole*）、《愿景》（*A Vision*）、《塔》（*The Tower*）和《也许是音乐和其他诗歌的歌词》（*Words for Music Perhaps and Other Poems*）。叶芝的诗歌吸纳了歌谣的特征，节奏柔和，旋律有点忧伤。

被请求写首战争诗

这年头,我想
诗人只应沉默
他们哪有能耐给政客正名
与百无聊赖的少女打趣
帮老人熬过漫漫冬夜
已让他们无暇他顾

1916年复活节[①] （节选）

太多的牺牲

会让心石头般硬

什么时候才算够?

注释

[①] 复活节：西方的重要节日，是纪念耶稣被钉于十字架受死后第三日复活的节日，亦称耶稣复活节、主复活节。在每年春分月圆后第一个星期日。由于每年的春分日都不固定，所以复活节的具体日期也不确定，大致在3月22日至4月25日之间。复活节的节日象征有复活节彩蛋和复活节兔。

一个爱尔兰飞行员预见了死亡[①]

我知道,在那高高的云端

我将结束此生

那些我捍卫的,我不爱

与之交战的,我不恨

我的故乡在基尔塔坦[②]

那里的穷人是我的同胞

无论结局怎样,他们都不受损伤

也不会更欢畅

我战斗,不为法律、不为责任

不为民众、不为赞扬

只是一时的冲动

驱使我去云端对抗

我权衡一切,想了又想

那未来的岁月不过是虚妄

过去的岁月也是虚妄

激越此生的只有死亡

注释

① 该诗被电影《孟菲斯美女号》引用。

② 基尔塔坦(Kiltartan):位于爱尔兰西部的高威。

约瑟夫·鲁德亚德·吉卜林
(Joseph Rudyard Kipling, 1865—1936)

英国第一位获得诺贝尔文学奖的作家。被视为短篇小说的革新者。

记者、作家和诗人。其文学创作横跨小说、诗歌，尤以短篇小说知名，被视为短篇小说的革新者。出生于当时的英殖民地印度孟买。父亲是孟买不列颠艺术学院的教授，母亲出身于牧师家庭。他的小说《丛林之书》(The Jungle Book)、《基姆》(Kim)和许多短篇小说等都得益于印度的生活经历。1871年吉卜林被送到英国接受教育。

1889年，开启了穿越中国、日本、美国，最终抵达伦敦的长途旅行。当他抵达伦敦时，发现他的小说已使他成为一名受欢迎的新星作家。在伦敦，他创作了许多故事和最著名的诗歌，如《东西方歌谣》(A Ballad of East and West)、《曼德勒》(Mandalay)和《英国国旗》(The English Flag)。1892年，与卡罗琳·巴莱斯蒂尔结婚，开启了他一生中最幸福的生活。随后，创作了《许多发明》(Many Inventions)、《丛林之书》(The Jungle Book)和《丛林之书续集》(The Second Jungle Book)、诗集《七海》(The Seven Seas)以及长篇航海小说《勇敢的船长》(Captains Courageous)等优秀作品。

1907年，成为英国第一位获得诺贝尔文学奖的作家。其颂扬孔武有力的军人气概的作品在第一次世界大战前夕鼓舞了众多青年踊跃从军，这也包括他的儿子约翰。17岁的儿子约翰起初因为视力弱被军队婉拒，凭着父亲的身份，最终成为一名步兵。到法国战场仅3个月后便战死。儿子的夭折使他一改帝国吹鼓手的立场，他咒骂战争，咒骂人世。战后，凭借自己的影响力，协同丘吉尔为阵亡士兵建造墓地。1936年去世后葬于伦敦的威斯敏斯特教堂，1937年出版自传《我的一些事》（*Something of Myself*）。1997年上映的电影《我的儿子杰克》叙述了吉卜林父子的人生。

两个加拿大纪念馆

1914-18

I

我们付出了一切,也赢得了一切
无须哀悼,也无须赞美
只需回忆
是恐惧,而不是死亡在杀戮

II

我们从遥远的国度奔赴此地
来拯救我们的荣誉和炮火连天的世界
我们长眠在这异国小镇
请相信,我们为你们赢得了世界!

我的儿子杰克[①]

"您可有我儿子杰克的消息?"
不在这一拨
"您觉着他什么时候会回来?"
不在这一拨,不随这班船

"您们有谁听说过他?"
不在这一拨
沉下去的难以再浮起
不在这一拨,不随这班船

"哦,天啊,究竟发生了什么?"
这一拨没有
任何一拨都没有
不随这班船,不跟那班船
只知他没让家族蒙羞

冲着这海风
冲着这海浪
昂起你高高的头
他是你的儿子
你把他献给了那海风、那海浪!

注释

① 杰克：吉卜林的儿子，名叫约翰·吉卜林。一战爆发后，受父亲的爱国主义和英国骑士精神的影响，在视力不合格的情形下依然奔赴战场（父亲出面协助），在法国营地过了自己18岁的生日。不久，在1915年9月27日的法国洛斯战役（5万多英军丧生）后失踪。心急如焚的父亲花了4年时间多方探问、寻找，未果，为纪念儿子写下这首诗。心力交瘁的他曾对妻子说，需要我跪下向你承认，是我杀死了我们唯一的儿子吗？他们的真实故事被拍成了电影《我的儿子杰克》。直到1992年，一个无名士兵的墓碑上才刻上了约翰·吉卜林的名字。2002年，一名军事史学家质疑其准确性。大量考查后，终确定。

常 态

1914-18

倘若有人问,我们为什么阵亡
告诉他们,只因我们的父辈在说谎

无名女尸

1914-18

没有头,也没有脚和手
令人毛骨悚然的漂浮的我终于靠岸了
我向所有母亲的儿子们乞求
因为我也曾是母亲

萨洛尼卡[①]墓地

1914−18

我观察了一千天了
挤出去,像乌龟一样缓缓地
爬进黑夜
现在我就学着乌龟的样
是狂热,而不是战斗——
是时间,而不是战役,在杀戮

注释
① 萨洛尼卡:希腊中北部的港口城市。

独　子

1914-18

我未杀掉任何人,却要了我母亲的命
她为我伤悲致死(临终还在为她的凶手祈祷)

在伦敦遭空袭

1914-18

在陆地在海洋,我满腹焦虑
我极力逃避征兵,但它弥漫在空气里

罗伯特·劳伦斯·比扬
（Robert Laurence Binyon，1869—1943）

他翻译的但丁的《神曲》深受埃兹拉·庞德、艾略特等人的赞赏。

英国诗人、剧作家和艺术史学家。因第一次世界大战期间创作诗歌《献给阵亡将士》（*For the Fallen*）而为人熟知。他翻译的但丁的《神曲》（*The Divine Comedy*）深得埃兹拉·庞德、艾略特等人的赞赏。

生于英国兰开斯特。从伦敦的圣保罗学校毕业后进入牛津大学的三一学院，在那里他的诗歌《珀耳塞福涅》（*Persephone*）获纽迪盖特奖。大学期间，出版自己的诗作。受桂冠诗人约翰·梅斯菲尔德主张诗歌应该大声朗诵的影响，开始对实验性的诗律感兴趣。

继第一本诗集《抒情诗》（*Lyric Poems*）出版后，又出版了两本关于绘画的书，即《17世纪的荷兰画集》（*Dutch Etchers of the Seventeenth Century*）和《约翰·克龙和约翰·赛尔·科特曼》（*John Crone and John Sell Cotman*）。后来出版的书籍如《远东绘画》（*Painting in the Far East*）和《龙的飞行》（*The Flight of the Dragon*）反映了比扬对中国、日本和印度三国艺术和文化的兴趣。

第一次世界大战的参战经历是他经典诗歌的主要灵感。他的经典战争诗有《运送伤员》（*Fetching the Wounded*）、《扇子》（*The Winnowing Fan*）、《铁砧》（*The Anvil*）、《起因》（*The Cause*）和《新世界》（*The New World*）等。

他战后的大部分时间在大英博物馆工作。1933年从大英博物馆退休后，获得了牛津大学名誉文学博士学位。同年跟随艾略特来到哈佛大学，成为哈佛大学的诺顿诗歌教授。还被任命为法国外籍兵团骑士、皇家学会会员，并在美国、中国、日本，以及欧洲的多所大学讲授艺术和文学。

其职业生涯长达50年。创作了诸多诗集和戏剧，两本历史传记和多本艺术史卷。在他生命的最后10年，还创作了《北极星和其他诗歌》（*The North Star and Other Poems*）、《燃烧的树叶》（*The Burning of the Leaves*）和未完成的《梅林的疯狂》（*The Madness of Merlin*）。剑桥大学教授约翰·哈奇认为，作为诗人，比扬的影响仅次于同时代的叶芝。

献给阵亡将士

母亲因优秀的孩子满怀感恩和骄傲
英格兰为她牺牲在异国他乡的孩子们哀悼
他们是母亲的骨肉,承载着母亲的精魂
为祖国母亲献身

庄严的鼓鸣,象征着他们死得光荣、神圣
响彻云天的哀歌
表达我们的缅怀
自豪在泪光里闪烁

年轻的他们唱着歌走向战场
身姿挺拔,眼神清澈,坚定洒脱
面对无法预知的命运
临危不惧,视死如归

当我们活着的人日渐衰老,他们永远年轻
时光也无法给他们增龄
每一次日升日落
我们都想起他们[①]

他们再也不能与战友欢笑嬉闹
再也不能坐上自家的餐桌

享受生活的日常
他们长眠在异国他乡

哪里有希望和梦想
哪里就能感受到他们迸发的力量
祖国铭记他们
就像夜晚熟知星星

如黑暗中的指路明灯
他们永驻我们心中
像那夜空中的星，即便我们成尘
他们依然闪耀在太空

注释

① 第四节屡屡被刻在世界各地的墓碑上。每年11月11日的阵亡将士纪念日，此诗节被人们吟诵。

夏洛特·玛丽·缪
（Charlotte Mary Mew，1869—1928）

托马斯·哈代认为她是同时代最优秀的女诗人。弗吉尼亚·伍尔夫赞扬她的诗作别具一格。

英国诗人，其作品跨越维多利亚时代和现代主义时代。1869年生于伦敦。

1894年在《黄皮书》上发表短篇小说《过往》（*Passed*）。20世纪初，定期向杂志投稿。她的第一本诗集《农夫的新娘》（*The Farmer's Bride*）于1916年以小册子的形式出版，该诗集1921年在美国由麦克米伦出版社以《周六市场》（*Saturday Market*）为题出版。作为诗人的她从此声名鹊起。

她试验性地使用了类似散文的长句，以及各种连词和缩进，这一独创性颇受赞誉。她经常从男性的角度创作。许多诗都采用戏剧性的独白形式。两首诗《肯》（*Ken*）和《在庇护所的路上》（*On the Asylum Road*）提到了精神疾病。诗作《树倒了》（*The Trees Are Down*）则是对生态保护的强烈呼吁。1927年妹妹死于癌症，抑郁的她被送入一家疗养院，后在那里自杀身亡。

无名战士纪念碑[①]

那无垠的田野还未再绿

就在昨天,青春的鲜血倾洒在那里

需一个墓地拥吻那肝脑涂地

尽管他们我们会时常自豪地想起,就像我们昂首阔步在这里

但壁炉边,孤寂的军属,已椎心泣血

我们将建纪念碑:在圆柱的顶端竖起带翼的胜利之神与和
　　平之神

在纪念碑下的台阶上——哦!一双展开的双手献上

代表春天的紫罗兰、玫瑰、月桂树和温馨的晶亮饰品

它们来自儿子或爱人的家乡

他们和数千个兄弟一道

为了至爱——祖国母亲

长眠此地:

睡在紫色、绿色、红色鲜花下的

都是年轻的生命:

看到这样一个蓬勃、绚烂的花床

孤母、遗孀们的心早已碎了!

但归根结底

上帝没被嘲笑,死者也没有

因为这墓碑将矗立在我们的交易市场——

在它的旁侧,谁在卖?谁在买?

　　(难道你我彼此

还将文绉绉地撒谎？）
审视着这市场上每个奔波忙碌的妓女们淫荡的嘴脸
和小贩们那讨价还价的充满奸诈的眉眼
这墓碑就是刚正不阿的上帝的脸

注释

① 该诗是作者的诗集《周六市场》里的最后一首。作者想表达战争结束了，士兵们的牺牲并没有被铭记，战争的受益者依然以邪恶的方式生活的观点。

约翰·麦克雷（John McCrae，1872—1918）

因爱国主义战争诗歌《在佛兰德斯战场》而声名远扬。

加拿大诗人、医生、艺术家和一战士兵。

生于安大略省圭尔夫市。16岁的麦克雷以优异的成绩被多伦多大学录取，由于哮喘病，经常休学。休学期间，在安大略农业大学任教。之后返回多伦多大学继续学习，1894年获得文学学士学位，后继续学习医学，1898年获得医学学士学位。在多伦多总医院驻院实习一年后，搬到巴尔的摩，在那里跟随奥斯勒学习。在南非（布尔）战争结束一段时间后，他回到蒙特利尔，担任蒙特利尔总医院的驻院病理学家。随后，他被任命为皇家维多利亚医院的医学副教授和蒙特利尔育婴堂和婴儿医院的病理学家。除了在麦吉尔大学和佛蒙特大学医学院讲授病理学之外，他还为《蒙特利尔医学杂志》和《美国医学科学杂志》撰写文章。

1914年第一次世界大战爆发后，应召入伍。1915年春，写下了在英语世界流传甚广的《在佛兰德斯战场》（*In Flanders Fields*），他也因此被铭记。

1918年1月28日，他因肺炎和脑膜炎去世。以极高的荣誉被安葬在法国海滨小镇维姆勒公墓，小镇的主要街道以他的姓氏命名为麦克雷街。他在加拿大圭尔夫的家被保存为博物馆。

在佛兰德斯战场[1]

在佛兰德斯战场,一行行

一排排的十字架旁

鲜红的罂粟花随风飘荡

告知世界 我们的鲜血洒在这异地他乡

天空中飞翔的云雀依然勇敢地歌唱

隆隆的枪炮声中听不到它们的歌声嘹亮

我们战死沙场

不久前,我们活着,感受黎明的曙光,凝望美丽的夕阳

我们曾爱和被爱着

而今我们长眠在佛兰德斯战场

继续战斗吧!从我们垂下的手里

接过火炬,把它高高擎起——

倘若我们的遗志被背弃

纵使罂粟花开遍佛兰德斯

我们也永不安息

注释

[1] 该诗创作于第二次伊普尔战役期间。这次战役中,德国使用了毒气,这是历史上第一次使用毒气的战役,造成大量伤亡。年轻的加拿大炮兵军官亚历克西斯·赫尔墨(1893—1915)不幸被德军炮弹炸死,因牧师当时在别地执行任务,葬礼便由麦克雷主持。从葬礼归来后,思绪万千的他写下了

在英语世界流传甚广的《在佛兰德斯战场》。该诗后来成为英语国家阵亡将士纪念日仪式上的固定诵读诗歌。受这首脍炙人口的诗歌的影响，后来英语国家的人们用手工制作的罂粟花纪念阵亡将士。在阵亡将士纪念日及前夕，佩戴罂粟花成了英语国家的一种习俗。

沃尔特·德·拉·梅尔
（Walter De La Mare，1873—1956）

T.S.艾略特在他75岁生日时，献诗《致沃尔特·德·拉·梅尔》。

英国诗人和小说家。生于肯特郡，曾在圣保罗大教堂唱诗班学校接受教育。从1890年起，在伦敦一家石油公司的统计部门工作，业余时间写作。1908年，在亨利·纽波特爵士的帮助下，获得一笔津贴，便专事写作。

1910年创作童话《三个毛拉·马尔加斯》（*The Three Mulla-Mulgars*），又名《三个皇家猴兄弟》（*The Three Royal Monkeys*）。文学史家朱莉娅·布里格斯称之为"被忽视的杰作"，评论家布莱恩·斯特布尔福德赞之为"经典的动物幻想小说"。此外，他也是一位著名的鬼故事作家。1921年，小说《一个侏儒的回忆》（*Memoirs of a Midget*）赢得了詹姆斯·泰特·布莱克小说纪念奖。1947年，他的《儿童故事集》（*Collected Stories for Children*）赢得了卡耐基儿童文学奖。

作为诗人，人们将他与托马斯·哈代和威廉·布莱克相提并论。作为短篇小说家，人们又将他比作亨利·詹姆斯。诗人W.H.奥登亲自为他编纂诗集。75岁生日时，T.S.艾略特为他献诗。

拿破仑

哦,士兵们,什么是世界?
我就是世界
我是这永不停歇的飞雪
是这北方的天空
士兵们,你们正穿行的
这荒野
就是我

罗伯特·塞维斯（Robert Service, 1874—1958）

凭借《拓荒者之歌》一举成名，享有"加拿大游吟诗人"的美名。

英裔加拿大诗人和作家。凭借《拓荒者之歌》（*Songs of Sourdough*）一举成名，享有"加拿大游吟诗人"的美名。

生于英格兰西北部，后随家人迁居到苏格兰的格拉斯哥，6岁开始写诗。年轻时受到吉卜林和史蒂文森的启发，怀揣发财与冒险的梦想，前往加拿大。

第一次世界大战爆发时，40岁的他试图入伍，但因身体状况被拒。曾为《多伦多星报》做有关战争的报道。

20世纪20年代，开始写惊悚小说。1922年出版《有毒的天堂，蒙特卡洛罗曼史》（*The Poisoned Paradise, A Romance of Monte Carlo*），1923年出版《钻工——大溪地的故事》（*The Roughneck. A Tale of Tahiti*），均被拍成无声电影。二战期间，为了鼓舞士气，好莱坞让住在加利福尼亚的他和其他名人到美国陆军营地朗诵他的诗歌，还被邀请在电影《破坏者》（*The Spoilers*）中扮演自己。在生命的最后几年，出版了6本诗集。创作了两卷自传——《月亮的农夫》（*Ploughman of the Moon*）和《天堂的哈珀》（*Harper of Heaven*）。

他声名远扬,被称为"加拿大的吉卜林"。1976年,加拿大专门为他发行了一枚邮票。怀特霍斯的一条主要街道罗伯特·塞维斯路(Robert Service Way)就是以他的名字命名的。

双胞胎[1]

约翰和詹姆斯是孪生兄弟
小镇起火时
约翰扑救詹姆斯的房子,奋不顾身
回过身,天呐,自己的宅子燃为灰烬

世界大战爆发
约翰踊跃报名当兵
部队里的他努力学投弹
家里的詹姆斯竟窃走了他的营生

丢了条腿的约翰告别战场
决心回乡自力更生
但得知女友成为詹姆斯的新欢
顿觉地转天旋!

时光飞逝。饱受打击的约翰隐忍苟活
与军队做生意的詹姆斯一夜暴富
一半的城镇成了他的
约翰呢?唉,可怜的他已入土,无人在乎

注释

[1] 该诗受托马斯·胡德诗歌《薄情的莎莉·布朗》的影响。

G.K.切斯特顿
（G. K. Chesterton，1874—1936）

被称为"悖论王子"。罗纳德·诺克斯说"我们这一代人都是在切斯特顿的影响下长大的"。

英国作家、文学评论家。被称为"悖论王子"。

生于伦敦。在圣保罗学校接受教育，随后进入伦敦大学斯莱德艺术学院学习，成为一名插画师。

一生著作颇丰，创作了80多本书，数百首诗，200多个短篇小说和数个剧本。是《每日新闻》《伦敦新闻画报》和《G.K.周刊》的专栏作家。其作品惯用悖论的方式，颇富机智和幽默感。《星期四男人》(The Man Who Was Thursday)是他最知名的小说。《布朗神父故事集》虚构了布朗神父（Father Brown）这个大侦探。关于辩证法的作品使一些不同意他观点的人也认识到《正统》(Orthodoxy)和《永恒的人》(The Everlasting Man)等作品的吸引力。

为《大英百科全书》撰写文章，关于狄更斯的纪实文学的见解在很大程度上促成了狄更斯作品在读者中的再次风靡，以及学者们对狄更斯的重新思考。他极大影响了圣雄甘地、赫伯特·乔治·威尔斯和英国桂冠诗人塞西尔·戴·刘易斯等。罗纳德·诺克斯在伦敦威斯敏斯特大教堂为他布道时说："我们这一代人都是在切斯特顿的影响下长大的。"

乡村庭院中的挽歌

为英格兰工作的人们
长眠在故土
英格兰的飞鸟和蜜蜂
围着他们的十字架起舞

为英格兰浴血奋战的人们
却像颗颗流星销匿
为了英格兰
他们在他乡安息

统治英格兰的人们
在开机密会议
为了英格兰
愿他们死无葬身之地

卡尔·桑德堡（Carl Sandburg，1878—1967）

"美国之声、美国力量和天才诗人。他就是美国。"

美国诗人、传记作家、记者和编辑。三次荣获普利策奖。他同先辈惠特曼一道，共同定义了什么才是体现美国精神、用美国语言书写的美国诗歌。代表作有《芝加哥诗集》（*Chicago Poems*）、《康胡斯人》（*Cornhuskers*）和《烟与钢》（*Smoke and Steel*）

生于伊利诺伊州的盖尔斯堡一个穷困潦倒的瑞士移民家庭，是铁匠之子。13岁时就离开学校打零工，帮助养家。美西战争期间，在波多黎各服役。服役期间，遇到了伦巴德学院的一名学生，这位年轻人说服了桑德堡战争后到伦巴德学院学习。

努力学习的他引起了菲利普·格林·莱特教授的注意，他不仅鼓励桑德堡写作，还花钱出版了他的第一本诗集《鲁莽的狂喜》（*Reckless Ecstasy*）。在伦巴德学院学习了4年，未获得毕业证书（后获得了伦巴德学院、诺克斯学院和西北大学的荣誉学位）。离开大学后，在密尔沃基遇到了摄影师爱德华·史泰钦的妹妹莉莲·史泰钦，两人喜结连理。之后夫妇俩搬至芝加哥，桑德堡在那里成为《芝加哥日报》的社论作家。哈里特·门罗在新创办的《诗歌杂志》上发表桑德堡的诗，并鼓励他继续以惠特曼式的诗歌风格写作。此时他被公认为是芝加哥文学复兴的一员（其他成员还有本·赫克特、西奥多·德莱塞、舍伍德·安德森和埃德加·李·马斯特斯等）。以《芝加哥诗集》（*Chicago Poems*）和《玉米人》（*Cornhuskers*）树立了其文学声望，并于1919年获得普利策奖。不久，创作了《烟与钢》（*Smoke and steel*），因其描写美国工业的自由诗而闻名遐迩。之后他开始对亚伯拉罕·林肯进行研究。《亚伯拉罕·林肯：草原岁月》（*Abraham Lincoln: The Prairie Years*）和《亚伯拉罕·林肯：战争年代》（*Abraham Lincoln: The War Years*）被认为是"关于林肯的最畅销、最有影响力的书籍"。

1932年出版了《玛丽·林肯，妻子和寡妇》（*Mary Lincoln, Wife and Widow*），4年后出版《是的，人民》（*The People，Yes*）。1950年，他因《诗词全集》（*Complete Poems*）再次荣获普利策奖。林登·约翰逊总统为桑德堡盖棺定论，说："卡尔·桑德堡不仅是美国之声、美国力量和天才诗人。他就是美国。" 2018年，在纽约的圣约翰大教堂入选美国诗人角。

美国远征军

亲爱的,多希望墙上挂着一把生锈的枪
枪的凹槽泛起片片铁锈
一只蜘蛛在它最黑暗、最温暖的角落
织一个银线窝
扳机和测距仪都生锈了
没有手去擦亮,枪就挂在墙上
食指和拇指不经意地指它一下
人们在近乎遗忘或渴望遗忘的情形下会提及这把生锈的枪
冲着蜘蛛说:接着织,很棒

草

在奥斯特里茨①和滑铁卢②，尸体被高高堆起
把它们铲平，我要工作——
我是草；我要覆盖一切

在葛底斯堡③，尸体被高高堆起
在伊普尔④和凡尔登⑤，尸体被高高堆起
把它们铲平，我要工作
多年后，乘客问售票员：
这是什么地方？
我们这是在哪儿？

我是草
我要工作

注释

① 奥斯特里茨：现捷克共和国的一个城镇。1805年这里爆发了世界战争史上著名的奥斯特里茨战役，又称三皇战役（法国皇帝拿破仑、俄罗斯皇帝亚历山大一世和神圣罗马帝国皇帝弗朗茨二世），这场战役奠定了拿破仑军事奇才的声望。

② 滑铁卢：比利时南部的一个城镇。这里1815年爆发了著名的滑铁卢战役。

③ 葛底斯堡：位于美国宾夕法尼亚州南部亚当斯县的一个自

治镇，是县政府所在地。这里爆发了美国南北战争中乃至北美大陆历史上规模最大、伤亡最惨重的一场战斗——葛底斯堡战役（1863年7月1—3日）。葛底斯堡战役被认为是内战的转折点，南方军队从此失去战略主动权，北方军队开始走向胜利。美国总统林肯在当地为阵亡将士修建的公墓揭幕典礼上，发表了他最著名的演讲——《葛底斯堡演讲》。

④ 伊普尔：比利时的一个城镇。这里第一次世界大战期间发生过惨烈的三次伊普尔战役。在第二次伊普尔战役期间，德军使用了毒气，这是历史上第一次使用毒气的战役，造成大量伤亡。第二次伊普尔战役期间，加拿大诗人约翰·麦克雷创作了爱国主义诗篇《在佛兰德斯战场》。

⑤ 凡尔登：位于法国东北部的一个城市。凡尔登战役是第一次世界大战中破坏性最大，时间最长的战役，造成了70多万人的伤亡。

他们照令执行

炸毁城镇
推倒墙垣
将工厂、教堂、仓库、家
毁为一堆堆遍布着石块、木屑和黑木橼的废墟
士兵们,我们命令你们

建城镇
垒墙垣
再将工厂、教堂、仓库、家
建成生活和工作的场子
工人市民们,我们命令你们

菲利普·爱德华·托马斯
(Philip Edwards Thomas,1878—1917)

被英国桂冠诗人泰德·休斯尊称为"我们所有人的父亲"。

英国诗人、散文家和小说家,也是一位战争诗人。

生于今伦敦南部的兰贝斯地区。曾在巴特西文法学校、圣保罗学校和牛津大学接受教育。1899年6月,还是一名大学生的他与海伦·贝勒尼斯·诺布尔结婚,决心靠写作为生。担任书评人的他每周评论多达15本书,曾在伦敦的《每日纪事报》担任文学评论员。

1913年发表小说《快乐的摩根人》(*The Happy-Go-Lucky Morgans*)。尽管托马斯认为诗歌是文学的最高形式,并经常评论诗歌,但他在1914年底才开始诗歌创作,最初以爱德华·伊斯塔维(Edward Eastaway)这个名字发表诗作。当时住在英国的美国诗人罗伯特·弗罗斯特鼓励他写诗。他们交往甚密,还计划一起到美国居住。弗罗斯特最有名的诗《未选择的路》(*The Road Not Taken*)的灵感正是来自与托马斯散步期间(当时托马斯对走哪条路犹豫不决)。

第一次世界大战爆发后,他应征参战,1916年11月被委任为皇家卫戍炮兵部队的少尉。1917年4月9日阵亡于阿拉斯战役,被葬于法国阿尼的英联邦战争墓地。

其诗歌经常以英国乡村为主题，有口语化的特点。短诗《纪念》（*Memoriam*）体现了他如何将战争和乡村主题融合在一起。他的诗作中至少有19首被格洛斯特的作曲家艾弗·格尼配乐。1985年11月11日，在威斯敏斯特教堂的诗人角，揭幕了一块纪念第一次世界大战期间阵亡的16位诗人的纪念碑，托马斯是被纪念者之一。仅两年多的时间里创作了140多首诗，其诗人生涯虽短，却在现代诗歌史上留下了浓重的一笔。英国桂冠诗人泰德·休斯尊其为"我们所有人的父亲"。

号　角

起床，起床
随号角的奏响
追逐男人的梦想
黎明将至
笼罩大地和水域的星光
即将隐匿
起床
驱散那露珠——
昨夜恋人们的足迹
驱散它，驱散它！

听
那嘹亮的号角
男人们，抛开一切
这新世界
神秘
又可爱
向天空睁开双眼
露水滋润的夜晚
风吹亮了星星的眼
和阳光一起起身
为这旷日持久的战争[①]

起床,起床!

注释

① 这里指持续了几年的第一次世界大战(1914—1918),诗人1915年志愿报名参军,1916年创作此诗,1917年阵亡。

这不是简单的对与错[1]

这不是政治家或哲学家

能判断的对错

我不讨厌德国人,也不会因为

对英国人的爱而头脑发热

去讨好报纸

除了讨厌那个肥胖的爱国者[2]

对威廉大帝[3]的怨恨是我的真爱——

他像个神,宣扬自己的世界观

但我不必在正义和非正义之间抉择

对于战争的争吵和喧嚣,我并不比风暴中

扫过树林的风了解更多

两个女巫的大锅[4]都沸腾咆哮着

德国的大锅预测,他们将所向披靡

美丽的英格兰预测的结果,如丧考妣

我无从知道,也不想知道

头脑愚笨的我会忽略史学家们

从废墟中搜罗的信息

涅槃的凤凰此时在他们的眼界之外冥想深思

和最优秀、最贫穷的英国人一道

我也高声哭喊,天佑英格兰

我们唯恐失去那些奴隶和牛群从未被赋予的东西

时代造就我们,造就了我们的国

我们了解、依赖、崇拜她
她如此美丽，一定要生生不息
我们是如此深爱着她
因为太爱自己，我们才仇恨敌人

注释

① 该诗创作于1915年12月26日，在托马斯与父亲发生激烈的争吵之后。父亲秉承报纸上的观点，认为德国人惨无人道，爱德华·托马斯不予苟同。此时的托马斯虽已在部队服役6个月，但仍驻扎在英伦。

② 那个肥胖的爱国者：有人猜测是指诗人的父亲。

③ 威廉大帝：德国皇帝、普鲁士国王，是维多利亚女王的长孙，因此也是英王乔治五世和俄国末代皇帝尼古拉二世的堂兄弟。

④ 女巫的大锅：正如莎士比亚的戏剧《麦克白》里女巫的大锅，可以预测未来。诗中的两口大锅：一口指英国，另一口指德国。

威尔弗里德·威尔逊·吉布森
(Wilfrid Wilson Gibson,1878—1962)

乔治亚诗歌运动的领导人之一。鲁伯特·布鲁克的挚友。

英国乔治亚时代的诗人、剧作家。生于诺森伯兰的哈克瑟姆,11岁开始写诗,未受过大学教育。1875年开始在杂志上发表诗作,1902年出版作品。《石板》(*The Stonefolds*)和《在门槛上》(*On The Threshold*)于1907年出版,次年又出版了诗集《生命之网》(*The Web of Life*)。1914年母亲去世后,前往伦敦发展。在伦敦,结识了爱德华·马什、拉塞尔斯·阿伯克龙比、约翰·君克沃特和鲁伯特·布鲁克等乔治亚派诗人,与他们一起创立了诗歌期刊《新编号》(*New Numbers*)。与鲁伯特·布鲁克成为挚友,后成为布鲁克的文学执行人。

写作生涯早期,创作了一些具有恐怖色彩的诗。第一次世界大战爆发前,在格洛斯特郡北部的迪莫克村与聚集在那里的诗人组成了迪莫克诗人团体,吉布森是该团体的创始人之一。1917年在英国服役期间,创作了不少优秀的战争诗歌。

早　餐

我们仰卧着吃早餐
炮弹从头顶呼啸而过
我用一片熏肉赌一块面包
赌赫尔联队将击败哈利法克斯队
当吉米·斯坦索普替换比利·布拉德福德打后卫时
金杰扬起头,接受了赌注,嘴里诅咒着
突然,他倒地,死了
我们仰卧着吃早餐
炮弹从头顶呼啸而过

信　息

"我记不清了……似乎五个
在战壕里，突然在我身边倒地死去，三个
临终时向我吐露他们的信息……"

从战场上下来的，死的比活的多
他完全聋了，茫然失措，膝盖骨折
步履蹒跚，喃喃自语：

"我记不清了……似乎五个
在战壕里，突然在我身边倒地死去，三个
临终时向我吐露他们的信息……"

"朋友们还在期待，想知道他们如何英勇杀敌
家人们耐心等待他们的消息
但是他们曾说了什么？他们的朋友家人是谁？无人知悉

"我记不清了……似乎五个
在战壕里，突然在我身边倒地死去，三个
临终时向我吐露他们的信息……"

华莱士·史蒂文斯（Wallace Stevens，1879—1955）

美国20世纪最受敬仰的诗人之一。被认为是"美国神话的重要组成部分。"

美国现代主义诗人、著名文学评论家和大师级的文体学家。

生于宾夕法尼亚州的雷丁市，父亲在家中为他提供了藏书丰富的图书馆，鼓励他阅读。少年的他就已学习了希腊文和拉丁文中的经典著作。中学时成绩优异，并展示出了写作才华。哈佛大学求学期间，在父亲的鼓励下，给哈佛大学文学期刊投稿，后成为期刊编辑，还荣获学院所有写作奖项。毕业后，成为一名记者。后进入纽约法学院学习，于1903年获得法律学位。1904年至1907年在纽约的几家律师事务所工作。1908年被聘为美国担保公司的律师。一次旅行中，结识了一个曾做过售货员、磨坊主和速记员的年轻女子艾尔西·维奥拉·卡切尔，不顾父母反对与其结婚。《纽约时报》曾报道："他的家人没有参加婚礼，他也再没有探望过他的父母……"

1917年，和妻子搬至法明顿大道210号，在那里完成了第一本诗集《风琴》（*Harmonium*）。1932年，在威斯特里台地118号购买了一栋20世纪20年代的殖民式建筑，后一直在此居住。作为30年代中期的一名保险主管，年收入2万美元，实现了财务自由。当时（大萧条时期）许多美国人都没有工作，在垃圾桶里寻找食物。1934年，被任命为公司的副总裁。

1947年，诗集《夏日的欢欣》（*Transport to Summer*）出版，《纽约时报》对该诗集给予了积极的评价。1950年发表了《秋天的极光》（*The Auroras of Autumn*），广受好评。晚年荣获多项文学大奖，诸如1951年的国家图书奖及1955年的普利策奖。哈佛大学向他提供了教职，被他婉拒。其最著名的诗作还包括《罐子的轶事》（*Anecdote of the Jar*）、《十点钟的幻灭》（*Disillusionment of Ten O'Clock*）、《冰激凌皇帝》（*The Emperor of Ice-Cream*）、《基韦斯特的秩序观念》（*The Idea of Order at Key West*）、《星期天的早晨》（*Sunday Morning*）、《雪人》（*The Snow Man*）和《看乌鸫的十三种方式》（*Thirteen Ways of Looking at a Blackbird*）。被哈罗德·布鲁姆赞为"我们这个时代最好的、最具有代表性的美国诗人"。还被认为是"美国神话的重要组成部分"。

阶段性

I
巴黎一个小广场
静待我们经过
人们懒洋洋地坐在那里
品酒

拐角处一辆马车
下雨了,雨季诉说着悲伤
曾经灰白的画面
添了绿叶

窗户里一只鹦鹉
看得见我们的游行队伍
听得到隆隆的军鼓声
还有小夜曲

II
这荣光颇具讽刺
不像
阿伽门农①的故事
只见
泥浆里的眼球和旁边被炸死的霍普金斯

平淡,苍白,血腥!

III
夜晚的军号
却像羽翼一样
安抚我们的心

刻有阿拉伯式花纹的蜡烛的烛光
在我们沉甸甸的梦里
摇曳

风在吹
鸢尾花在风中摇摆

欢天喜地的飞鸟
在夜的深渊里歌唱

结有黄色果实的藤蔓
沿着墙壁
垂下
那里连着地狱

IV
高贵的死神再一次

美化了最平凡的人

温克尔倒下时

感受到了

阿伽门农临终时的骄傲

伦敦的劳作与荒废

能给予他

什么——

将他献祭给那苦涩的荣光?

伦敦的悲苦

能带来什么——

给那稍纵即逝的胜利沉痛一击?

注释

① 阿伽门农:古希腊神话中的迈锡尼王国国王,特洛伊战争中的希腊联军统帅,领导联军攻克特洛伊城,取得辉煌的胜利。但妻子克吕泰涅斯特拉对阿伽门农出征时以长女伊菲革涅亚献祭之事怀恨在心。在他荣归故里时,与情人埃癸斯托斯合谋将其谋杀。

萨拉·蒂斯代尔（Sara Teasdale，1884—1933）

因诗集《情歌》获得普利策奖。

20世纪杰出的美国浪漫派女诗人，因1917年出版的诗集《情歌》（*Love Songs*）获普利策奖。

生于密苏里州一殷实人家。少时因健康状况不佳，在家接受教育。1904年到1907年，是"陶艺家"（The Potters）的成员之一，其成员是一群十几岁到二十几岁的女艺术家，她们在圣路易斯创办了艺术和文学月刊《陶艺家之轮》。1907年在当地一家报纸《里迪镜报》发表第一首诗。同年出版她的第一本诗集《致杜塞的十四行诗和其他诗歌》（*Sonnets to Duse and Other Poems*）。1911年出版第二本诗集《特洛伊的海伦和其他诗歌》（*Helen of Troy and Other Poems*），该诗集受到评论家的好评。1914年与她作品的崇拜者恩斯特·菲尔辛格喜结连理。1915年出版第三本诗集《通往大海的河流》（*Rivers to the Sea*），该诗集非常畅销，多次重印。1916年，夫妇俩搬至纽约中央公园西区。丈夫不断出差，聚少离多的二人最终离婚。1933年，服安眠药自杀身亡。

作为诗人的她一直被认为是歌者。

战时的春天

总觉春天还很远很远
叶芽的芬芳很淡很淡
春天啊,你怎忍心来到
这悲惨世界
这苦难人间?

太阳北移,白昼变长
长庚星迟迟不亮
白日怎踟蹰不去
放纵人们打仗
不停歇地打仗?

遍地野草在苏醒
风吹草长,渐渐起伏如浪
野草啊,你怎忍心摇曳于
大地之上
那新的墓场?

苹果树下曾走过对对情侣
苹果花会再次绽放
情人们可安然无恙?
死神让他们阴阳相隔
死神啊,你多么张狂

埃兹拉·庞德（Ezra Pound，1885—1972）

发掘、提携了乔伊斯、艾略特、海明威等作家。对于19世纪末或20世纪初的诗人来说，不受庞德的影响仿佛是"遭遇一场暴风雪却未感到凉意"。

美国诗人、评论家，20世纪英美诗坛的巨匠，早期现代主义诗歌运动的代表人物。作品包括《还击》（*Ripostes*）、《休·塞尔温·毛伯利》（*Hugh Selwyn Mauberley*）和史诗《诗章》（*The Cantos*）。

生于美国爱达荷州的小城海莱市。1905年毕业于汉密尔顿学院，次年获宾夕法尼亚大学比较文学硕士学位。后在印第安纳州一所大学任教，因作风问题被开除，此后一直旅居欧洲。

庞德对诗歌的贡献始于20世纪初，在发展意象主义方面发挥了重要作用。他在伦敦担任几家美国文学杂志的外国编辑，帮助发掘和塑造了文学界新人，曾帮助詹姆斯·乔伊斯出版《一个青年艺术家的肖像》（*A Portrait of the Artist as a Young Man*）和《尤利西斯》（*Ulysses*），帮艾略特修改《荒原》（*The Waste Land*），并向出版社推荐。在巴黎结识并帮助海明威出版了第一本书。海明威1932年写道，对于19世纪末或20世纪初的诗人来说，不受庞德的影响仿佛是"遭遇一场暴风雪却未感到凉意"。

第二次世界大战期间,被驻意大利的美国军队以叛国罪逮捕。关押期间,开始创作《诗章》(*The Cantos*),1948年出版《比萨诗章》(*The Pisan Cantos*),1949年被美国国会图书馆授予博林根诗歌奖,引起巨大争议。经过作家同行的奔走,1958年获释,后一直在意大利生活,死后葬在他心爱的意大利。作为争议最大的人物之一,同时也是英美文学现代运动的核心人物,学术界对其作品的研究热情迄今有增无减。

休·塞尔温·毛伯利① （节选）

三
法律上，人人平等。
摆脱了佩西斯特拉托斯②
我们选了一个无赖或者说是太监
来统治我们

一个英明的阿波罗③

无法再现
什么样的神、什么样的人或什么样的英雄
我愿敬上一个锡花环④呢？

四
无论如何，有人奋勇战斗⑤，
有些人相信是为了祖国母亲，无论如何……

有些人迅速武装
有些人出于探险
有些人不愿示弱
有些人害怕被指责
有些人出于对杀戮的热爱，想象着
稍后学习……

有些人在恐惧中逐渐爱上杀戮；
"为国捐躯，无上荣光"⑥，绝非事实

因为听信了老人的谎言
到地狱深处感受了一遭，然后不再相信
便回了家，回到谎言的家
诸多谎言的发源地
旧谎言和新恶行的家

高利贷由来已久
和公共场合下的骗子

前所未有的大胆，前所未有的耗费
年轻的生命和高贵的血统
白皙的脸颊，漂亮的身体

前所未有的坚韧

前所未有的坦率
从未被告知的幻灭
战壕里的歇斯底里和忏悔
死肚皮发出的令人毛骨悚然的惨笑

五

死亡无数

死的都是他们中最优秀的

为了一条无用的老狗

为了一个拙劣的文明

漂亮嘴巴上的微笑，真美

曾经的明眸在泥土下阖上

就为了两个破塑像

为了几千本破书

……

注释

① 全诗被认为是庞德的自传诗，是他与伦敦的告别曲。表达了诗人对现代文明、现代文化的鄙视及对士兵们为维护它而投身、牺牲于第一次世界大战的痛惜与不值。

② 佩西斯特拉托斯：古代雅典的暴君。

③ 阿波罗：希腊神话中宙斯之子、太阳神和司掌文艺之神。主管光明、音乐、诗歌、医药、畜牧等。被认为是消灾解难之神，也是人类文明、迁徙和航海者的保护神。是古希腊艺术中男性美的象征，俊美且富有才华的他受到了众多女神的欢迎。诗中指英明的领导人。

④ 锡花环：人们经常将花环献给胜利者。锡花环指用回收

的锡罐制作环保花环，花环上的"花朵和叶子"是由各种饮料锡罐上的材质切割而来，并使用花线和铜线缠绕成圆形花环。此文里提到的锡花环远不及金花环珍贵，暗示诗人对当下境况的不满。

⑤ 这里指让众多精英献身的第一次世界大战。

⑥ 出自古罗马诗人贺拉斯的诗句。

西格弗里德·萨松（Siegfried Sassoon，1886—1967）

他的现实主义战争诗歌引起了极大争议。

英国诗人、小说家，同时也是军人。

出生于英格兰肯特郡一个富裕的犹太家庭。在剑桥大学克莱尔学院学习历史，未获得学位。生活优渥的他业余时间喜欢写诗和狩猎。第一部作品《水仙花杀手》（*The Daffodil Murderer*）是模仿英国桂冠诗人约翰·梅斯菲尔德的《永恒的仁慈》。

第一次世界大战爆发后自愿参军。1915年底在法国参战，战场上表现得异常英勇，屡建功勋，绰号为"疯狂的杰克"。但是，战场上的残酷景象和战友的阵亡让他深深体会到战争带来的祸害。1917年受伤后，给陆军部写了一封公开信《士兵宣言》，拒绝继续战斗。他在信中写道："我认为那些有能力结束这场战争的人在故意延长战争。"在伯特兰·罗素的敦促下，下议院宣读了这封信。本应被军事法庭审判的他因诗人罗伯特·格雷夫斯的介入（辩称萨松患有弹震症，需要治疗）而住院治疗。

因其一战诗歌被熟知。《反攻及其他诗歌》（*Counter-Attack and Other Poems*）收集了他最好的战争诗歌，玛格丽特·麦克道尔在《文学传记词典》中写到，所有这些诗都是"对现实犀利的悲叹或讽刺"。之后的诗集《西格弗里德·萨松的战争诗》(*The War Poems of Siegfried Sassoon*) 收录了64首战争诗歌,大部分创作于住院期间,诗歌描绘了战争的残酷和血腥,表明了他的反战立场。公众对萨松的诗歌反应激烈,一些读者抱怨诗人缺乏爱国主义精神,而另一些读者则认为他对战争现场的描述过于极端,细节过于逼真。《泰晤士报文学增刊》的一位评论家则说:"他的战争诗之所以有活力,是因为在冷嘲热讽的诗行间隐藏着一种强烈的情感。"麦克道尔在《英国诗歌史》写道:"(萨松)之所以被铭记是因为他的100多首战争诗歌,字里行间一直反对一战的继续。"

战后,萨松参与工党的政治活动,发表反战演讲,同时继续写作。先后出版小说《猎狐人回忆录》(*Memoirs of a Fox Hunting Man*) 和《步兵军官回忆录》(*Memoirs of an Infantry Officer*),共和党的一位评论家赞扬《猎狐人回忆录》为"一部内容清新的小说",美国小说家、记者罗伯特·利特尔称其为"一本独特的、异常美丽的书"。他的自传体小说《乔治·谢斯顿回忆录》(*The Memoirs of George Sherston*) 三部曲为他赢来一片赞誉,统称为"谢思顿三部曲",作品也叙述了他的反战情绪。

1957年,皈依天主教。在皈依之前的一段时间,他的写作主题已与宗教有关。德里克·斯坦福在《书籍与学者》一书中称他的宗教诗歌集《序列》(*Sequences*) 中的诗歌"是本世纪最棒的宗教诗歌所不可或缺的一部分"。其宗教诗歌逊色于战争诗歌。读萨松的战争诗就像翻阅一本完整的战争史,它们记录了参战者从激情到幻灭再到反战的过程。

要紧吗？

要紧吗——失去一条腿？……
人们都心存善意
当他们狩猎归来
狼吞虎咽地吃下松饼和鸡蛋时
你不必在意

要紧吗——失去了视力？……
有许多盲人能干的活
人们都心存善意
当坐在阳台上的你想起往昔
你可以把脸向光亮转去

要紧吗——那战壕里的噩梦？……
为了忘却，你不妨以醉解忧
人们不会说你疯了
他们知道你是为国而战
没人会介意

无用的司令部军官

当秃顶、碌碌无为的我心情烦躁
我就与大红脸的上校待在司令部
敦促闷闷不乐的英雄们战死在前线
我则在高级酒店狂吃豪饮
腆着肥胖暴躁的脸,念阵亡榜单
"可怜的小伙子"我会说"我以前与他父亲很熟悉
是的,最后关头我们损失惨重"
战争结束时,年轻人都战死了
我则摇摇晃晃地返回家中
寿终正寝

于我体内,过去、现在、将来会集

于我体内,过去、现在、将来会集
他们各执一词,争吵不息
欲望执掌现在
将理性绞杀
情爱则越过未来的藩篱
舞动不息

于我体内,野人拥抱先知
头戴花冠的文艺神阿波罗
冲着充耳不闻的亚伯拉罕[1]高歌
于我体内,猛虎细嗅蔷薇[2]
审视我的内心,朋友,你会战栗
因为那也是你的内心

注释

[1] 亚伯拉罕:传说中古希伯来民族和阿拉伯民族的共同祖先。他代表忠诚、顺从和传统。

[2] 于我体内,猛虎细嗅蔷薇:诗人萨松著名的诗句,原文:In me the tiger sniffs the rose. 这里借用了余光中先生的绝佳翻译——"心有猛虎,细嗅蔷薇"。

致所有阵亡的军官

天堂什么情况？希望你愿意讲
希望你别来无恙
告诉我，你找到永恒的白昼了吗？
还是被吸进了漫漫长夜？
我闭眼时，你表现得稀松平常
我听到你讲了几句老笑话——
虽然你在黑暗里巡逻。
但你的形象在我脑海浮现

你憎恨战壕之旅
想享受美好时光
你渴望回家，渴望和无忧无虑的朋友相聚
渴望和他们一样，享受和平环境下的时光和工作
一切都不可能了。你出局了：
你不可能再爬回人间
架起机枪扫射的你——
却被一颗哑弹袭击

不知为何，我坚信你会完蛋
因为你如此渴望活：
竭尽全力保命，保护你的肌肤
知道这个世界需要大的付出

你冲着炮弹开玩笑,还像往常一样谈"购物"
你习惯讲脏话,骂得酣畅
你说"耶稣基督!什么时候是个头?
三年……如果我们突破不了防线,可真生不如死"

当他们告诉我你被留下等死
我不愿相信,但觉得一定是真的
接下来的一周,血淋淋的光荣榜会说你
"受伤和失踪"——他们一贯这么干
当奄奄一息的士兵被留在弹坑里等死时
除了寂寥的天空和疼痛的伤口,还能有什么
当他们呻吟着要水喝,才知道
时值黑夜,他们根本不该苏醒!

再见,老伙计!代我向上帝问好
告诉他我们的政客们发誓
他们决不退缩,直到普鲁士政权①被踩在
英格兰的铁蹄下……你还在听吗?……
是的……战争至少两年内不会结束
但是我们已死了很多很多人……我被泪水模糊的双眼
凝视着黑暗。加油!
希望他们杀你时杀得顺手

注释

① 普鲁士政权：1701年1月18日，腓特烈三世在哥尼斯堡加冕成为普鲁士国王腓特烈一世，并从此开始了普鲁士王国两百多年的显赫历史。到1786年腓特烈二世去世时，普鲁士已经成为欧洲强国之一，其行政机构的高效率和廉洁为欧洲之首。威廉一世于1871年1月18日，即普鲁士王国成立170周年纪念日，在法国凡尔赛宫登基称帝，宣布建立以普鲁士王国为首的德意志帝国，即所谓的德意志第二帝国。普鲁士历史从此并入德意志帝国历史。1918年11月7日，柏林爆发革命，要求德皇退位。在比利时征战的威廉二世得知革命爆发后，试图仅放弃德意志皇帝头衔，保留普鲁士国王称号，但为避免发生更大变乱，德国总理马克斯·冯·巴登亲王于11月9日午前宣布德皇已经退位，并于同日将首相职务移交德国社会民主党领袖弗里德里希·艾伯特。威廉二世流亡荷兰，德意志帝国及普鲁士王国灭亡。

临终时刻

昏睡中的他意识到周围一片死寂
那死寂像无法晃动的坚固的墙
似水的死寂像漂浮的琥珀色光线
在睡眠的羽翼里飞翔和震颤
静默平安；他生命的彼岸
被向内的、没有月光的死亡之波浸淹

有人把水喂他嘴里
他咽下去，没有挣扎；呻吟着
从血色的绝望倒向黑暗
忘却了那抽鸦片后的悸动和伤口的疼痛
水——静静的，那在堰上滑动的绿色
水——让他的船行在明亮的小巷
那里有鸟鸣，有花香
和颤动的夏日光亮：顺流而下
他心满意足地放下桨，叹口气，睡了

夜里，病房里刮来一阵风
把窗帘吹得满是褶皱
夜里。他失明了
看不见星星在流云中幽灵般地闪烁
紫色，红色，绿色，奇怪的各色斑点

在他失明的眼睛里闪烁,然后褪去

雨——他听见雨在黑暗中沙沙作响
听见温润与冷傲交织的雨的浅吟低唱
温柔的雨拍打着低垂的玫瑰;啪嗒啪嗒的阵雨
浸透了树林;席卷而来的不是雷鸣后的暴雨
而是细细的宁静
轻轻的,慢慢的,把生命冲走

他动了动,翻了下身;疼痛
像一个徘徊已久的野兽,突然跃起
用尖爪和利牙抓住、撕裂他的幻梦
有人在他身边;当悲催的时刻终于过去
躺着的他不停地战栗
死神走过来把他凝视

多点些灯,围在他床边
借给他你的眼、温热的血和活下去的意志
和他说话,唤醒他;也许你能救他
他很年轻,他讨厌战争。当残忍的老竞选者稳操胜
　　券时
他怎么能死?

但死神回答:"我选择他。"

所以他去了。夏夜寂静无声
静默平安，睡神的面纱
远处传来砰砰的枪声

令人痛苦的战争经历

来点上蜡烛：一支，两支；飞来一只飞蛾；
多么愚蠢的乞丐，这样误入
用荣光、液体火焰炙烤他们的翅膀——
不，不，不是那样——想到战争不大好
否则你一整天压抑着的想法就跑出来吓你
士兵们已经被证明没有疯
除非他们抑制不住那可怕的思绪
那思绪会驱使他们到树林里胡言乱语

把烟斗点燃；看，多稳的手
深吸一口；不再思考；数到十五
你感觉对极了……
为什么不下雨？……
我希望今晚有一场雷阵雨
用满满一桶水来冲洗这黑暗
让玫瑰垂下那淋湿的头

书籍；它们是多么快乐的一群啊
安静、耐心地站在架子上
身着暗褐色、黑色、白色、绿色等各种颜色
你会读哪个？
坦率地讲；哦，一定要读点什么；它们都很棒

我告诉你

世界上所有的智慧

都在书架上等着你

而你却坐着啃你的指甲,抽你的烟斗,聆听这静寂:

天花板上一只晕头转向的飞蛾在扑腾

在屋外令人窒息的空气里

花园在等待一些被延误的东西

树林里一定有成群的鬼魂

他们不是在战斗中牺牲的人——牺牲者葬在法国——

裹尸布裹着的可怕的尸体——他们是寿终正寝的老人

灵魂丑陋

他们因罪恶感而空耗自己

安适慈和的你在家静享明媚的夏日

你绝想不到曾有一场血腥的战争!

是的,你会的……为什么,你能听到枪声

听。砰,砰,砰——相当柔和……却从未停息——

那些低语的枪声——哦,上帝,我想出去

我要冲他们尖叫,让他们停下来——我要疯了

因为这枪声,我简直、完全要疯了

宽　恕

大地上的悲苦让眼睛不忍直视
除非美丽遍布各处
战争是祸根,却让我们理性
为自由而战,我们解脱了

对负伤的恐惧、对仇敌的愤慨以及心仪的东西的失去
一切都必须接受
我们是快乐军团,我们知道
时间不过是那掠过草地的金色的风

还有一个小时就要辞别
我们和你们一样热爱的世界
同志们,兄弟们,我们的内心毫不掩饰
我们更需要什么

梦想家

士兵是死神王国里的子民
他们没有明天
他们临危受命
每人都承载着各自的伤楚、国仇和家恨
士兵们宣誓英勇战斗，他们必须奋不顾身
在激烈的战斗中获胜
士兵们是梦想家：当枪声响起
浮现在他们脑海里的是燃着炉火的家、整洁的床铺、自己
　　的妻

在肮脏的防空洞里遭老鼠啃咬的他们
在被淫雨冲塌的战壕里
想着用球棒击球的快乐
想着休公休假、看电影、与家人斗嘴
坐着通勤车去上班
林林总总，他们的想法都被嗤为黄粱梦

"他们"

"当孩子们从战场归来,他们将不同以往。"
主教说得慷慨激昂
"为了正义,勇敢的他们给予敌人猛烈的打击
他们战友的鲜血赢得
我们光荣民族的新契机
勇敢的他们与死亡殊死较量。"

男孩们回答,"我们的确都大不一样!
乔治失去了双腿;比尔失明
可怜的吉姆,肺部中弹,痛不欲生
伯特得了梅毒……您根本找不到任何一名
上了战场却一如以往的士兵"
主教叹息:"上帝的旨意不可思议!"

在战壕里自杀

我认识一个新兵,朴实天真
军旅生活单调,他报以微笑
在旷野孤寂的黑夜,他酣然入睡
每天随早起歌唱的云雀,吹着口哨

冬日的战壕极度压抑,令人恐惧
满是面包屑、虱子,却没有酒
他用枪射穿自己的头颅
从此无人提及

欢呼的人群,热情洋溢
夹道欢迎战士荣归故里
怎知道他们溜回家中默默祈祷
怎知道那消失在战壕里的青春和欢笑

鲁伯特·布鲁克（Rupert Brooke，1887—1915）

获得诺贝尔文学奖的爱尔兰诗人叶芝称他为"英伦最英俊的男孩"。

英国诗人，因其帅气的外表和在第一次世界大战期间创作的爱国主义战争诗歌《士兵》（The Soldier）而闻名。被获得诺贝尔文学奖的爱尔兰诗人叶芝称为"英伦最英俊的男孩"。

生于英格兰沃里克郡的拉格比小城。自小天资聪明，1906年，进入剑桥大学国王学院学习古典文学。1907年，年仅26岁的哥哥迪克死于肺炎，为抚慰父母丧子之苦欲搁置学业，但父母坚持要他返回大学。

3年的校园生活让他结识了许多文人、艺术家，成为布鲁姆斯伯里作家群中的一员。弗吉尼亚·伍尔夫告诉薇塔·萨克维尔·韦斯特，她曾与布鲁克在月光下的剑桥拜伦池裸泳。他还加入了另一个被称为乔治亚诗人的文学团体，同时也是迪莫克诗人中重要的一员，该群体还包括罗伯特·弗罗斯特和爱德华·托马斯。

1912年，遭遇严重情感危机的他为了疗伤，先后去了德国、美国和南太平洋。《蒂亚雷塔希提岛》（Tiare Tahiti）和《伟大的爱人》（The Great Lover）创作于旅行中。期间为《威斯敏斯特公报》撰写旅行日记。他乘船穿越太平洋，在南洋停留数月。人们后来发现他可能与一个名叫塔塔玛塔的大溪地女人孕育了一个女儿。

第一次世界大战爆发后，在爱国主义热潮和英雄主义的激励下积极报名参军。1915年2月随英国地中海远征军出征，休整期间，创作了他最著名的战争诗歌。这些诗歌都采用了短小精悍的十四行诗形式。不幸的是他因被蚊子叮咬感染，患上败血症，英年早逝，应验了他的诗行，葬于异国他乡。《泰晤士文学增刊》1915年3月11日发表了他的两首十四行诗《死者》（*The Deceased*）和《士兵》（*The Soldier*）。圣保罗大教堂的主教复活节时在教堂讲坛上诵读了《士兵》，并称："再也无法找出更高贵的方式来表达纯洁而高尚的爱国主义精神了。"温斯顿·丘吉尔在讣告中给予了他极高的评价，说："鲁伯特·布鲁克留下了无与伦比的诗歌……这些诗歌是鲁伯特·布鲁克本人全部的历史和写照。"其最著名的诗集《1914年及其他诗歌》（*1914 and Other Poems*）于1915年5月首次出版。

士　兵

如果我死了，请如是记住我：
异国他乡的某个角落将永属英格兰[①]
那富饶的土壤里
将蕴含一粒更肥沃的尘土
一粒在英格兰出生、长大，获得心智的尘土
这是一具曾欣赏过英格兰的鲜花，徜徉在英格兰的小径
呼吸过英格兰的空气
接受了家乡河流的洗涤
沐浴过家乡太阳，属于英格兰的身体
请相信，他的心会远离一切邪恶
他那永恒的精神力量，会不遗余力
把英格兰赋予的思想散播到所及之地
传播英格兰的视野、声音及美好的梦想
分享朋友间爽朗的笑声和英格兰天空下内心的宁静和安详

注释

[①] 在布鲁克的家乡英国拉哥比市他的塑像下，镌刻着该诗的前两行："如果我死了，请如是记住我：/异国他乡的某个角落将永属英格兰。"

逝 者

人生的起伏跌宕使他们悲欣交集
岁月让他们心存善意
目睹过日出日落,各种色彩他们都感知过
聆听过音乐,经历过动荡
感受过甜蜜的梦乡和梦醒后的清爽
他们爱过,曾兴奋地缔结友谊;感受过惊喜,享受过独处
抚摸过鲜花、毛皮和爱人的脸
但一切不再继续

被变换的风吹笑了的水面
在郎朗晴空下闪闪发亮
冰霜之神大手一挥
凝固了生机勃勃的雀跃的水波
那白茫茫的光亮——永恒的荣光
夜幕下洋溢着无限的宁静和安祥

伊丽莎白·达里尤什（Elizabeth Daryush，1887—1977）

父亲是桂冠诗人罗伯特·布里奇。

英国诗人。生于英国伯克郡，原名伊丽莎白·布里奇。父亲是桂冠诗人罗伯特·布里奇。她早期的两本诗集《仁慈》（*Charitessi*）和《诗歌》（*Verses*）以伊丽莎白·布里奇的名字出版。35岁嫁给阿波斯人里·阿克巴·达里尤什，两人一起在波斯生活了4年。她的诗歌风格继承了父亲的诗风，作品主题多是批评上层阶级及其特权给他人带来的不公。

唐纳德·戴维在《达里尤什诗集》（*Daryush's Collected Poems*）的序言中写道："在20世纪的文学史里，未能找到伊丽莎白·达里尤什，这将会是我们面临的最有力、最可悲的指控之一。"评论家芬利说"她的诗歌激怒了那些热衷于艾略特、庞德的新诗歌风格的读者，他们仅倾情于现代主义和意象主义的诗歌，而无视其他诗风"。他评论道："对于那些希望全面探索英语诗歌的读者来说，不应该忽视伊丽莎白·达里尤什诗歌的优秀之处。"

献给美索不达米亚战役[①]的幸存者

战争毁掉的时代是寸草不生的沙海
经历的人都知道

在毁灭一切的咆哮声中
野秃鹫在盘旋，还有贪欲和卑微的恐惧
那里还潜伏着饥饿、疾病、痛苦
残忍的它们在等待时机
它们将所有生的美丽从一个个肢体上剥离
把其当作愚蠢碾碎在荒原上的乱石里

沙漠：那些人和你们一样
是战争的祭品——战神的信徒
（他们忍受着残酷的折磨
压抑着恐惧和罪责）
他们深悉战争恶魔般闪电的凝视
为屁大的事将他们永远毁灭

注释

① 美索不达米亚战役：指1914年至1918年，即第一次世界大战期间，奥斯曼帝国与德国结盟后，英国为夺取奥斯曼帝国控制的波斯油田而发动的战争。英国及其盟军印度军队与奥斯曼帝国在美索不达米亚，即现在的伊拉克地区展开交战。

经过艰难险阻,英军最终于1917年3月占领巴格达。漫长的战斗异常艰苦,许多人死于疾病和恶劣的气候。1918年10月30日,奥斯曼土耳其帝国向英国投降。

艾伦·西格（Alan Seeger，1888—1916）

被称为"美国的鲁伯特·布鲁克"。其代表作《我和死亡有个约会》是约翰·肯尼迪总统的最爱。

美国战争诗人。被称为"美国的鲁伯特·布鲁克"。

生于纽约市，家境优渥。在哈佛大学求学期间开始写诗，在期刊发表。1910年获得哈佛大学学士学位。法、德两国开战后，出于对法国的热爱，自愿加入法国外籍军团参战，他敬仰英国骑士的优秀代表菲利普·锡德尼，愿意为荣誉而战。1916年阵亡于索姆河战役。

他最著名的诗歌《我和死亡有个约会》（*I Have a Rendezvous with Death*）创作于1916年冬天克里夫科尔的露营中。诗歌表达作者不惧死亡，视死亡为荣誉的斯多葛派哲思。

1923年7月4日，法国国务委员会主席雷蒙·普恩加莱在合众国广场为第一次世界大战中自愿为法国战斗的美国人献上了一座纪念碑。纪念碑基座上的青铜雕像是由让·布夏以西格的照片为灵感设计的，基座的背面刻有西格及其他23名牺牲的法国外籍军团士兵的名字。雕像底座的两侧刻有西格去世前不久写的诗《纪念为法国牺牲的美国志愿者》（*Ode in Memory of the American Volunteers Fallen for France*）的两节。1970年，法国比亚里茨的一条街道以他的名字命名。

我和死亡有个约会[1]

我和死亡有个约会
在防御工事周围
当春天携着斑驳的树影回归
空气里弥漫着苹果花的香味
天空湛蓝，春光明媚
我和死亡有个约会

也许死亡会拉起我的手
带我走进他黑暗的领地
合上我的眼皮，止住我的呼吸——
也许我会从他身边悄然离去
当春光再次明媚
草地繁华似锦
在某一个饱受战火的山坡，弹痕累累
我和死亡有个约会

想念家里床铺上的丝绸枕头
羽绒被散发着香味
床笫间，相爱的人彼此相依
脉搏贴脉搏，呼吸融呼吸
床笫间，相爱的人一起苏醒在夜的静寂……
而我和死亡有个约会

当这北方的小镇再次春光明媚

在一个炮火连天的深夜

我将信守诺言

毅然赴会

注释

① 该诗深得美国总统约翰·肯尼迪的喜爱。

艾弗·格尼（Ivor Gurney，1890—1937）

不仅是诗人，还是作曲家，因音乐作品而闻名。

英国诗人、作曲家。创作了300多首歌曲，因音乐作品而闻名。

生于英格兰格洛斯特。父亲是一位裁缝，他的教父是当地牧师，一直鼓励他追求艺术和创作。在教父的图书馆里阅读了大量书籍，后获得皇家音乐学院的奖学金，因第一次世界大战的爆发而中断学业。

因视力不好1917年才得以入伍，在法国战事中两次受伤（第二次是毒气）。第一次世界大战期间开始写诗，并把诗作寄回英国出版。他的第一部诗集《塞文与索姆》（*Severn and Somme*）和第二部诗集《战争的余烬》（*Sar's Ember*）都反映了他的战争经历和对格洛斯特乡村的热爱。战后他回到皇家音乐学院跟随拉尔夫·沃恩·威廉斯学习。战前曾有精神崩溃经历的他行为日益怪异，后再次离开学校。1922年被送进精神病院，在那里度过了余生，卒于肺结核。

作品被大量收藏，也一直再版。其中有《最好的诗及其创作过程》（*Best Poems and the Book of Five Makings*）、《80首左右的诗》（*80 Poems Or So*）、《奇迹的奖赏：伦敦、科茨沃尔德和法国的诗歌》（*Rewards of Wonder: Poems of London, Cotswold and France*）

和《诗集》（*Collected Poems*）。其信件由安东尼·博登编辑，以《黑夜中的星星：艾佛·格尼写给查普曼家族的信》（*Stars in a Dark Night: The Letters from Ivor Gurney to the Chapman Family*）为题出版。

2014年4月，BBC四台播出了一部关于艾弗·格尼的纪录片，题为《热爱战争的诗人》。

致他的爱人

他走了,我们之前所有的计划
都破产了
我们不会再去科茨沃尔德①漫步
羊儿静静地在那儿吃草
谁也不理会

你不知道
他有多敏捷
在蓝天下的塞文河②上
驾驶着我们的小船
疾驰

你再也见不到他了
他死了
死得很崇高
用骄傲的紫罗兰盖上他
用塞文河边那高贵的紫色

盖上,快盖上他!
用一层厚厚的缅怀之花③——
遮住那红色的血迹
无论怎样

那些，我必须忘记

注释

① 科茨沃尔德：小镇名。位于英格兰格洛斯特郡，莎士比亚家乡的南面。

② 塞文河：英国境内最长的河流，全长约354千米（220英里）。发源于威尔士中东部坎布里亚山脉最高点普林利蒙，流经威尔士和英格兰（在什鲁斯伯里附近穿越英格兰边境），向南注入大西洋的布里斯托尔湾。

③ 缅怀之花：在讲英语的国家，缅怀之花指用来悼念阵亡将士的红色罂粟花。

艾萨克·罗森伯格（Isaac Rosenberg，1890—1918）

一战中阵亡的3位重要诗人之一。

英国诗人和艺术家。他的《战壕里的诗》（*Poems from the Trenches*）被公认是第一次世界大战期间创作的最杰出的诗歌之一。

生于布里斯托尔。1912年出版了一本10首诗的小册子《夜与日》（*Night and Day*）。1915年3月，出版了第二本诗集《青春》（*Youth*）。因长期找不到工作，于1915年10月应征入伍。他在一封个人信件中表达了对战争的态度："我从来不是因为爱国的原因参军。什么也不能成为战争的借口……"随部队被派往法国西线服役，在战壕里继续写诗，包括《战壕中的破晓》（*Break of Day in the Trenches*）、《返回时我们听到云雀歌唱》（*Returning We Hear the Larks*）和《死人堆》（*Dead Man's Dump*）。

因德军1918年3月21日在西线展开进攻，随所在部队奔赴前线之前，将最后一封信及诗歌《度过这些苍凉的日子》（*Through These Pale Cold Days*）寄回英国，不久后遇难。罗伯特·格雷夫斯在他的《告别一切》一书中把他描述为"一战中阵亡的3位重要诗人之一"（另外两位是欧文和索利）。

运兵船

荒诞的拥挤
像杂技演员一样地弯曲
昏睡的灵魂
我们以各种方式躺着
却无法入睡
潮湿的风阴冷
蹒跚的人们太粗心
如果你打个盹
风或男人的脚
就会割到你脸上

理查德·奥尔丁顿（Richard Aldington，1892—1962）

以评论家和传记作家的身份闻名于世。

英国作家和诗人，也是意象派运动的早期成员。

生于朴次茅斯。在多佛学院及伦敦大学接受教育。后成为一名记者，并开始在英国的杂志上发表诗歌。1911年，与布里吉特·帕特莫尔有过一段恋情。通过她，结识了美国诗人埃兹拉·庞德和诗人希尔达·杜利特尔。后与希尔达结婚。之后夫妇俩认识了富有影响力的美国诗人艾米·洛厄尔，洛厄尔将他们介绍给作家D.H.劳伦斯，后者成为了两人的挚友和导师。奥尔丁顿的诗歌有意象派特征，他倡导带有鲜明形象的极简主义自由诗。庞德将他的3首诗推荐给哈里特·门罗的《诗歌》杂志发表。1914年至1916年期间奥尔丁顿担任《自大者》杂志的文学编辑和专栏作家。

1916年6月入伍。1917年被任命为皇家苏塞克斯团的少尉。1919年2月复员。他可能从未从战争创伤中完全恢复，在《战争图像》（*Images of War*）和《欲望图像》（*Images of Desire*）两本诗集中描述自己的战场经历。《流放和其他诗歌》（*Exile and Other Poems*）也涉及战争创伤。1929年发表了半自传体战争小说《英雄之死》（*Death of a Hero*）。乔治·奥威尔称之为最棒的战争小说。和这一时期出版的其他关于战争的小说一样，《英雄之死》也深受审查制度的影响，但他没有修改或删减小说，而是用星号代替了敏感词语，希望唤起人们对出版商审查制度的关注。1930年，出版了《十日谈》(*The Decameron*)的译本和战争故事集《通往荣耀之路》(*Roads to Glory*)，随后又出版了小说《所有人都是敌人》(*All Men are Enemies*)。

1942年，与新婚妻子移居美国后，开始写传记，后以评论家和传记作家的身份闻名。1943年出版了《惠灵顿公爵：惠灵顿公爵一世亚瑟·韦尔斯利的生平和成就》(*Wellington: The Duke: Being an Account of the Life & Achievements of Arthur Wellesley, 1st Duke of Wellington*)，1950年出版了《劳伦斯：一个天才的肖像，但……》(*D. H. Lawrence: Portrait of a Genius, But ...*)，随后又出版了《罗伯特·路易斯·史蒂文森：一个叛逆者的肖像》(*Robert Louis Stevenson: Portrait of a Rebel*)，以及1955年的《托马斯·爱德华·劳伦斯：阿拉伯劳伦斯的传记调查》(*T. E. Lawrence:Lawrence of Arabia: A Biographical Inquiry*)。他最后一部重要作品是关于普罗旺斯诗人和诺贝尔文学奖得主弗雷德里克·米斯特拉尔的传记。

他被认为是优秀的战争诗人之一，在威斯敏斯特教堂的诗人角，为纪念一战中阵亡的诗人而立的纪念碑上的16位诗人名单，他是其中之一。

战争叫嚣

美国!
英格兰的厚脸皮小弟
在邦克山①等地
血腥地突袭你可敬的大哥
(我们的历史书中从未提及),
关于战争或和平,我能告诉你什么?
说,您忘记了1861吗?
忘记了在牛奔河②,葛底斯堡,弗雷德里克斯堡③?
你们死了一百万人?
告诉我,
那是你一生最伟大
抑或最灾难性的时刻?
谁知道?你不知;我也不知
谁能知晓战争的结局?
说,乔纳森兄弟④,
你可知这是怎么回事?
让我悄悄告诉你一个没被提及的秘密:
我们都在和平中待得太久了
或许还不知道和平有多好,
所以我们驻扎此地,
而且想赢……

真不错，成为了士兵

被负责征兵的军士接收了

训练，配备制服和枪支

跟女友说再见

然后上前线

吹着口哨："到蒂珀雷里⑤的路长着呢。"

背负91磅的负荷

每天行进40英里已是不错

粗茶淡饭、手脚起泡、疲惫不堪、身体受伤

饥渴难耐，恶魔一样地战斗

（乔纳森兄弟，大家都和你我一样）

用马克西姆⑥机关枪扫射

弹片尖叫着呼啸而过

榴弹炮像皮卡迪利街⑦的交通一样嗡嗡作响。

文明？

乔纳森兄弟，如果你能听到

他们口中吹的《马赛曲》或《穿过佐治亚》⑧的口哨

您也想去

每天两万步，乔纳森兄弟！

也许您们比我们更文明，

也许我们只是暂时忘记了文明，

也许我们真的为和平而战

毕竟，今后的生活会更有趣——

对于诗人和画家来说更有趣——
当欢呼声停息
掩埋了死人
其余的人都重返工作
无论那工作是关于诗人的字词还是画家的颜色
他们的工作会更有趣

毕竟,总有战争,总有和平
战争总是人群的战争
和平总是艺术的和平

即使现在
战争如巨浪在头顶拍击
像狂风和洪水般地咆哮
海神仍在绘制红色海藻叶的图案
为了琉喀忒亚®和忒提斯®
还将琥珀切成颈链
即使现在
当《马赛曲》像受伤的女人一样尖叫
巴黎(城市里的低俗之地)恐惧不安
但诗人们仍在创作
没人听的歌
之前也鲜有人听过

众多的人们遵循着这样的原则

和平时期相互较量

战争时期相互较量

遇到冲突

他们就在那高踞岩石上的艺术城堡里

用金铜锤制他们的梦

用松木、帕罗斯岛⑪大理石和蜡雕刻他们的梦

和着废旧乐器奏出的刺耳音乐

唱着甜美荒诞的歌曲

他们很惬意

但岩石上艺术家们的小城堡

总是被骚扰

尽管那里有美丽和寂静

但总有眼泪，饥饿和绝望

不过那座小城堡一直坚守着

对抗世界上所有的战争

就像英国，乔纳森兄弟

不会在这场伟大的战争中倒下去

总有战争，总有和平

战争总是人群的战争

和平总是艺术的和平

注释

① 邦克山：美国波士顿附近最高的山坡之一（高出地面11英尺），美国独立战争期间英美两国曾激烈交战的地方。

② 牛奔河：位于弗吉尼亚州东北部的一条小溪，美国内战期间曾在此进行过两场战斗。第一次牛奔河战役也称第一次马纳萨斯战役，于1861年7月21日发生在弗吉尼亚的马纳萨斯和牛奔河附近，是南北战争中的第一场重大战役，也是当时美国历史上规模最大、最血腥的战役。南方军队在杰克逊卓越的指挥下粉碎了北方军队剑指里士满的攻势。北方民众对他们的军队的第一次牛奔河战役的失败感到震惊，因为他们普遍认为北方军队会在战役中轻松获胜。13个月后杰克逊在同一地点的第二次马纳萨斯战役中再次大败北方军队。双方都很快意识到，这场战争会比他们想象的更漫长、更残酷。

③ 弗雷德里克斯堡：美国得克萨斯州基利斯比县中部的一座城市，是基利斯比县政府所在地。弗雷德里克斯堡于1846年由普鲁士人奥特弗里德·汉斯·冯·梅斯伯男爵建立，以当时的普鲁士王子弗雷德里克威廉三世中的名字命名小镇名。梅斯伯男爵开明地管理此镇，其知名度攀升。当时的许多居民都是德国移民，他们的母语是德语，开始时大多数人拒绝学习英语，拒绝拥有奴隶，在南北战争中反对脱离联邦。

④ 乔纳森兄弟：新英格兰的化身。他因周报*Brother Jonathan*和幽默杂志*Yankee Notions*而广受欢迎。在新英格兰以外的社论漫画和爱国海报中，乔纳森兄弟通常被描绘成一个啰嗦的新英格兰人，穿着条纹裤子、黑色外套，戴着烟斗帽。在新

英格兰境内，则被描绘成一位有进取心、活跃的商人。

⑤ 蒂珀雷里：爱尔兰最大的内陆县，以其牧场和牧马闻名遐迩。

⑥ 马克西姆：即马克西姆机枪，第一支全自动机枪，由当时居住在英国的工程师兼发明家海勒姆·马克西姆于1884年左右发明。后被各大国在战争中使用。因为此武器，第一次世界大战有了"机枪战争"的绰号。

⑦ 皮卡迪利街：位于英国伦敦区威斯敏斯特自治市的一条街道，地处梅菲尔以南，西与海德公园相接。

⑧《穿过佐治亚》：美国南北战争时期北方军队的军歌。后在美国南方之外的地方广为传播。电影《飘》引用了此曲。

⑨ 琉喀忒亚：海中女神，善良美丽，乐意救助遇险的水手。传说只要遇见她，就会有好运。当奥德修斯的木筏被波塞冬摧毁时，她前来援助，用她的浮力披肩将他安全包裹起来。罗马人将她视为女神玛特·玛图塔。

⑩ 忒提斯：古希腊神话中的海中仙女，是50个海洋仙女的非官方领袖，英雄阿喀琉斯之母。传说她握着阿喀琉斯的脚踝把他放在斯提克斯河里浸泡，故其全身不被兵刃所伤，被她手握的脚踝没能泡到冥河水而成为其弱点。

⑪ 帕罗斯岛：爱琴海中部基克拉泽斯群岛的一个希腊岛屿。帕罗斯岛现是欧洲最受欢迎的旅游热点之一，以其精美白色大理石闻名中外。

战壕诗

我们坐在战壕里
他坐在
昨晚吹起的一块冻土块上
我坐在一个未爆炸的弹壳上
像流亡者一样,我们抽烟、聊天
我们聊到令人神往的伦敦:
聊到伦敦的女人、餐馆、夜总会、剧院
此时此刻的伦敦
出租车正载着人们奔赴晚宴……
机枪扫射护墙时
我们沉默了一会

他说:
　"我来这里差不多两年
只看到一个人毙命。"

"有点蹊跷"

"子弹击中他的喉咙
倒在火堆里的他
大喊'上帝啊!我要死了!'"

"天哪,真可怕!"

"嗯,我去年在这里的工作
是最不堪的
晚上要到那边铁丝网上
取回牺牲战士身上的胸牌
他们已挂在那里六个月了
最糟糕的是
他们的尸体一碰即碎
我们看不到他们的脸,谢天谢地
他们都戴着防毒面具……"

我不禁打个冷战:
"这里太冷了,咱们挪个地?"

威尔弗雷德·欧文（Wilfred Owen，1893—1918）

最著名的战争诗人（战争诗人有时特指参加过第一次世界大战的诗人）。

英国诗人和军人。最受尊敬的战争诗人之一。

生于英格兰什罗普郡。从小对文学艺术感兴趣，十几岁开始写诗。1911年，被伦敦大学录取，但未能获得奖学金，期间他在牛津郡做了一年的牧师助理。1913年，在法国的伯利茨英语学校教书。1915年回国，加入艺术家步兵团。1916年被任命为曼彻斯特军团的少尉。

1917年，战斗中受伤的他被送往爱丁堡附近的克雷格洛克哈特战争医院。在那里，他遇到诗人西格弗里德·萨松。萨松作为他的导师，将他介绍给了罗伯特·格雷夫斯和赫伯特·乔治·威尔斯。住院期间，他写下了许多经典诗歌，包括《青春挽歌》（*Anthem for Doomed Youth*）、《为国捐躯》（*Dulce et Decorum Est*）、《麻木》（*Insensibility*）、《徒劳》（*Futility*）、《春季攻势》（*Spring Offensive*）和《奇怪的相遇》（*Strange Meeting*）等。他的诗歌深受导师西格弗里德·萨松的影响，逼真地描述了战争的残酷、恐怖，质问战争的意义，痛斥鼓动战争者的虚伪。

1918年6月，返回军团。因在战争中的英勇表现被授予了军功十字勋章。1918年11月4日，在战争结束前的一个礼拜在奥尔斯带领部下横渡桑布雷-瓦兹运河时遭机关枪扫射阵亡，时年25岁。当他的死讯传至他的故乡时，当地的教堂钟声刚好宣布战争结束。欧文的诗集《威尔弗雷德·欧文诗集》由萨松选录、作序，1920年12月出版。

　　1985年11月11日阵亡将士纪念日，在威斯敏斯特教堂的诗人角，揭幕了为纪念一战中阵亡的16位诗人而立的纪念碑，碑文是威尔弗雷德·欧文的文字："我的主题是战争，和战争的遗憾。我用诗歌表达遗憾。"欧文的战争诗歌影响深远，他及他的诗歌衍生出了众多的电影、戏剧、纪录片。

奇怪的相遇[①]

我似乎从战斗中逃脱了
顺着昏暗的隧道,挖穿了
激烈的战事中被炸起的花岗岩

却邂逅蜷缩在那里的一些人,他们呻吟着
想得太快或死得太快,都追悔莫及
当我刺向他们时,一个人跳起
他坚定的眼睛以幽怨的眼神盯着我
举起痛苦的手,他仿佛在祝福
他的微笑,他死一般的微笑让我察觉
这里是阴沉之地,我们站在地狱里

他的脸因巨大的恐惧显得格外粗糙
没有血液抵达那里
这儿没有砰砰的枪声,也听不到浓烟呛出的呻吟声
"陌生的朋友,"我说,"在此没有理由哀悼。"
"的确"对方说,"除了我们未竟的青春岁月,唉……
不管你有什么梦想
那也是我的;我也一直在追求世界上
最激动人心的美丽
它不在平静的眼神里,也不在编织的发辫里
它在嘲笑稳定运行的时间

如果梦想会悲伤，它比此时更伤悲。
因为当我欢喜，许多人已经大笑了
当我哭泣，那消失的东西早已远去
我指的是不为人知的真相
是战争的悲情和战争孕育的悲情
现在人们会对我们破坏的东西满意了
抑或不满意，因为沸腾的热血更使冤冤相报，鲜血横流
应战方会像母老虎一样迅速残忍地反扑
没有人愿意抗议，即使参战国都举步维艰
曾经的我勇敢地奔赴前线
也富有智慧
为了不让世界大倒退
不让它沦为庞大的难民营
当战争机器使得尸横遍野
我要奋勇向前，告知人们真相
即使真相被掩盖、扭曲
我也会竭尽全力
但不是通过创伤；也不是战争
男人们的血已经流干了"

"我的朋友，我是你杀死的敌人
我在这黑暗里认出了你
因为昨天你捅我、杀我时，一直眉头紧皱
我躲闪着。但我的手冰冷、无力

现在让我们一起安息……"

注释

① 该诗标题引自雪莱的诗歌《伊斯兰教起义》(*The Revolt of Islam*)里的诗句。

无　效

移他到太阳下吧——
温柔的阳光曾让他苏醒
家里，他种了一半的田地在窃窃私语
倘若不是今天早上这场雪
阳光定能将他唤醒，即使在法国
现在什么能唤醒他
和善的太阳公公也未必知晓

想想阳光是怎样唤醒种子的——
阳光曾唤醒了冰冷星球上的黏土，使生命不息
他修长的四肢，富有弹性，现在依然温热
难道太阳不能将他唤醒
而让新的坟头堆起？
——啊，是什么让辛勤的阳光
惊扰泥土的安息？

自　残[①]

> 我会安慰国王
> 安慰困境中的他
> 因为有人决心去牺牲
> 但是那个厌恶服从纪律
> 和不遵守秩序的人
> 我不能哀悼他
>
> ——叶芝

I　序言

他们拍着小伙的背膀告别，坚定地告诉他
应该向匈奴人永远展示一张坚毅的脸
父亲宁愿他死，也不愿因他蒙羞
骄傲地看着他走了，父亲很高兴
他的母亲呜咽着说出她的担忧
直到他挂了彩，因一个不致命的伤口需要休养时，母亲才
　　放心
姐妹们希望女孩也能射击、冲锋、咒骂……
小兄弟——寄去他最喜欢的香烟
每周，每月，他们都给他写同样的信，
以为他待在某个年轻人的工棚里，趴在枪托上写信
因为他是这么说的

他说他一小时错失一次攻击目标
姑娘们取笑他太迟钝
他的视力渐渐模糊，冻僵的手无缚鸡之力
勇气像沙袋里的沙子
经历风雨后，漏了
受伤，发烧，战壕足，休克
从未远离他。但也未将悲惨的他置于死地
为了让中弹后瘫在那里的他饱受折磨
为了强权们胡作非为，死神依然克制着

夜间，他看见士兵们开枪打自己的手
他们的家人从来不知晓。似乎有点卑劣
"宁死不丢脸，这就是风格！"
父亲这样说

II　行动/场景

那个黎明，巡逻队
抬着他。这次，死神没有放过他。
他们除了给他擦咳出的血，别无他法
难道是意外？——步枪走火了……
没被狙击？没有。（他们后来发现了英国地雷）

III 诗歌

面对绵绵无期的苦役
和布满电网的无法破防的漆黑的壕沟墙
他失去了理智
四周的火帘、头顶的火舌慢慢吞噬着
却未立刻把他烧死
等待他的只有死亡和嘲弄
活着的希望只有一半,生和死都令他烦躁

IV 尾声

他们把他与他吻过的枪一起埋了
如实地写信给他母亲,"蒂姆笑着走了"。

注释

① 诗歌原标题是 S. I. W.,即 *Self-Inflicted Wounds*. 据报道,因为恐惧和精神压力,第一次世界大战中或战后,英法士兵中的自杀或自残现象很严重。因自杀或自残死去的士兵不被追加任何荣誉。

为国捐躯[①]

身子弯得像沉重麻袋包下的老乞丐，
我们一边咒骂，一边老太婆似地咳嗽
一边屈膝从泥泞中挪出
面对那挥之不去的照明弹，我们转过身去
艰难地跋涉，不知何时才能歇息
昏昏欲睡的我们疲乏地行进着。许多人丢了靴子
有的被鞋磨破了脚，步履蹒跚。腿迈不动，眼看不见
晕头转向；连不远处的毒气弹的轰鸣声也充耳不闻

毒气弹！毒气弹！快跑，孩子们！——一阵骚乱
急忙戴上那粗糙的面具
一些人在尖叫，跌跌撞撞
仿佛是在烈火或热石灰里苦苦挣扎……
透过蒙蒙雾霾和深绿色的光
我仿佛在绿色的海面下，看着他溺亡

梦里的我总是不知所措
他扑向我，被呛溺的他奄奄一息

假如你也在那令人窒息的梦里，你也会跟在
他被抛了进去的货车后面
你也会看到他的眼白在脸上转动

也会看到他那吊死鬼的脸恶魔一样可怖
假若你能听见每一次的颠簸
血从肺泡破裂的肺叶中喷出
那肺叶癌细胞一样可怖,喷出的血和恶心的反刍物一样苦
还有无辜的舌头上那不可治愈的溃疡
我的朋友,你就不再会激情洋溢地
向满腔热血的孩子们宣讲
那古老的谎言:为国捐躯
　　　　　无上荣光[2]

注释

① 该诗在电影《重生》中被引用。

② 最后两句引自古罗马诗人贺拉斯。

青春挽歌[①]

什么样的丧钟为那哑畜般惨死的士兵敲响?
唯有那短枪残忍的怒吼
唯有那长枪时断时续的嗒嗒
在重复着它们急促的祈祷

没有颂扬,没有祷告,没有哀悼,没有丧钟
只有子弹刺耳的呼啸声、炮弹疯狂的爆炸声
为他们号啕悲哭
嘹亮的军号声还命令着来自各地的他们奋勇

我们能点燃什么样的烛光为他们送终?
那神圣辞别的光亮未在男孩们手里擎起
却闪烁于他们晶莹的泪光里

为他们送终的女孩们脸裹尸布般的苍白
坟头的鲜花是满腔的隐忍
每一个日暮,他们的亲人都拉上窗帘默哀

注释

① 该诗在电影《重生》中被提及。

玛格丽特·伊莎贝尔·科尔夫人
（Dame Margaret Isabel Postgate Cole DBE，1893—1980）

1970年被授予DBE勋章，成为一名贵族。

英国社会主义政治家、作家和诗人，出生于英国剑桥的一个知识分子家庭。父亲曾在剑桥大学三一学院执教，本人曾在剑桥大学罗丁公学和格顿学院接受教育。在格顿学院，阅读了H·G·威尔斯、萧伯纳等人的作品，阅读了关于社会主义的书籍后，开始质疑陪伴自己成长的英国国教，接受了社会主义。

完成所修课程后（剑桥大学直到1947年才允许女性正式毕业），成为圣保罗女子学校的古典文学教师。第一次世界大战期间，其弟拒服兵役而被监禁。她由此产生了和平主义的信念。她的诗歌《落叶》（*The Falling Leaves*）是对第一次世界大战的回应。在随后的反对征兵运动中，结识了后来的丈夫科尔，两人合著了几部侦探小说。

20世纪30年代初，鉴于德国和奥地利政府对社会主义运动的镇压以及西班牙的内战，放弃了和平主义。从1952年起担任伦敦郡议会的市议员直到1965年该议会被废除。1965年被授予OBE勋章。1970年因对地方政府和教育的贡献被授予DBE勋章。

落 叶

今天,当我骑马经过
看到大片棕色的树叶从树上飘落
时值午后,四周一片静寂
没有呼啸的风将树叶旋到天空
树叶却纷纷悄然飘落
就像雪花抹去了中午
目睹此景
我不禁想起了英雄的他们
此刻已凋零
岁月和瘟疫不再侵蚀他们
正值青春飞扬的他们
却如同飘落在佛兰德粘土[①]上的雪花

注释

① 佛兰德粘土:佛兰德斯战场是第一次世界大战中最残酷的战场。作者用佛兰德粘土(The Flemish Clay)一词旨在抗议无意义的战争。

老　兵

见到他时，他正端坐在阳光下
失去双眼的他离开了战场
越过栅栏，一群手捧鲜花的新兵前来拜访
咨询他的战斗经验
他说说这，谈谈那，还给他们讲故事
未提及他脑海里的噩梦
听到我们在旁侧，他说：
"可怜的孩子，他们怎能体悟那绝望？"
目睹端坐着的他
转动着他空空的眼窝
我们中的一个忍不住问："你多大？"
"5月3日刚满十九。"

多萝西·帕克（Dorothy Parker,1893—1967）

美国邮政总局在她诞辰99周年纪念日发行了一枚印有她头像的29美分纪念邮票。2005年其出生地新泽西海岸被指定为美国国家文学地标。

美国诗人、作家和评论家。生于新泽西州。幼时丧母，叔叔马丁·罗斯柴尔德于1912年因乘泰坦尼克号遇难。父亲次年去世。童年的她就读于一所天主教文法学校，后求学于新泽西州莫里斯顿。1914年，把自己的第一首诗售给《名利场》杂志。22岁时，在《时尚》杂志谋到一份编辑工作。1917年加盟《名利场》，担任戏剧评论家。同年，嫁给了股票经纪人埃德温·帕克，1928年离婚。1919年，成为阿尔贡金圆桌会议（一个非正式的作家协会，他们在阿尔贡金酒店共进午餐）的创始成员。1922年，在《聪明集》发表了她的第一部短篇小说《如此漂亮的小图片》（*Such a Pretty Little Picture*）。1925年《纽约客》创刊，被列入编委会。多年来，以"忠实读者"的身份发表诗歌、小说和书评。1926年出版第一本诗集《足够的绳索》（*Enough Rope*），颇为畅销。随后出版了《日落之枪》（*Sunset Gun*）和《死亡与税收》（*Death and Taxes*）两个系列。1930年出版小说集《生者的哀歌》（*Laments for the Living*）。

1929年，以自传体短篇小说《大金发》（*Big Blonde*）获得欧·亨利奖。1934年，与演员兼作家艾伦·坎贝尔结婚，夫妇俩移居洛杉矶，组成了一个高薪的编剧团队。他们为米高梅和派拉蒙公司创作了诸多佳作，其中1937年《一个明星的诞生》（*A Star Is Born*）获得了奥斯卡奖提名。

  1963年成为洛杉矶加利福尼亚州立学院的客座教授。几年后，因心脏病发作死于纽约的一家酒店。作为民权的坚定信徒，她将自己的文学遗产遗赠给了马丁·路德·金。数月后，马丁·路德·金遇刺，遗产移交给了全国有色人种协进会（NAACP）。1992年8月22日，美国邮政总局在她诞辰99周年纪念日，发行了一枚印有她头像的29美分的纪念邮票。1996年，在阿尔贡金圆桌会议成员的努力下，美国图书馆之友将该酒店指定为国家文学地标。2005年其出生地新泽西海岸被美国图书馆之友指定为国家文学地标。2014年，入选新泽西州名人堂。

老 兵

年轻时,我胆大强壮
哦,对就是对!错就是错!
我的羽翼舒展,我的旗帜飘扬
我骑着马去给这个世界纠错
我高喊:"出来吧,狗杂种,来干一仗!"
为只有一次死的机会而悲泣

现在我老了,好与坏
被织在怪异的方格纹里
坐着的我慨叹:"世界就这样。
明智的人听任一切
赢一场,输一场
孩子,无妨。"

惯性驱使着我,我困惑不解
这就是所谓哲学

梅·韦德伯恩·坎南

（May Wedderburn Cannan，1893—1973）

她的诗《鲁昂》被婉拒桂冠诗人头衔的菲利普·拉金收录在《牛津20世纪英语诗集》中。

英国诗人。曾在牛津大学出版社辅助父亲工作，后在巴黎的战争事务部间谍部门工作。

战时和战后共出版3本诗集：《战争时期》（*In War Time*）、献给贝维尔·奎勒·库奇的《辉煌的日子》（*The Splendid Days*）和献给她父亲的《希望之家》（*The House of Hope*）。1934年出版小说《孤独的一代》（*The Lonely Generation*）。她的诗《鲁昂》被婉拒桂冠诗人头衔的菲利普·拉金收录在《牛津20世纪英语诗集》（*Oxford Book of Twentieth Century English Verse*）中。虽然在20世纪20年代停止写作，但在人生暮年完成了自传体作品《灰色的幽灵和声音》（*Grey Ghosts and Voices*）。她的曾侄女夏洛特·芬在《战争的眼泪》（*The Tears of War*）中出版了更多坎南未发表的诗歌，该书还通过摘录坎南的自传和未婚夫写给坎南的信讲述他们的爱情故事。其未婚夫在一战中阵亡。

1914年8月

太阳从起伏的山后升起
空荡的四周仅余下收割的干草
一只黑鸟窗边鸣叫
女孩跪下祈祷：
　"主啊，您曾整夜保佑他。
求您白天依然保佑他。"

太阳升到炮弹掠过的高度
枪炮已备好
奋战了一晚的士兵
又继续白天的忙碌
子弹在护墙旁呼啸
钻进新翻的泥土

太阳缓缓沉到山后
干草被运走
一只黑鸟窗边鸣叫
女孩跪下祈祷：
　"主啊，您曾整夜保佑他。
求您白天依然保佑他。"

太阳从炮弹扫过的高度缓缓下沉

枪炮已摧毁目标
但那晚，睡下的那个士兵
再也没醒来迎接黎明
一只黑鸟从窗边飞逃
女孩跪下祈祷

战　后

战后，也许我会再坐在
和你曾坐过的阳台
看群山倚着湛蓝的天
静静地坐到夏日的午后

想起
我们美好的过往，我伤心不已
唯愿他人就是你
像从前那样唤我的名字

薇拉·布里坦(Vera Brittain, 1893—1970)

作为一个和平主义者,她因在《轰炸大屠杀》一书中公开反对对德国城市的轰炸而受到诽谤。

英国作家、女权主义者、社会主义者、和平主义者。

出生于英国的纽卡斯尔安德莱姆。唯一的哥哥爱德华是她成长过程中最亲密的伙伴。她不顾父亲反对,在牛津的萨默维尔学院攻读了英国文学。第一次世界大战期间担任志愿援助分遣队护士,在伦敦、马耳他和法国工作。她的未婚夫罗兰·奥布里·莱顿、好友维克托·理查森、杰弗里·瑟洛和哥哥爱德华都在第一次世界大战中阵亡。他们之间的书信被收录于《迷惘的一代的信函》(Letters from a Lost Generation)一书。第二次世界大战期间,开始创作《给和平主义者的信》(Letters to Peace Lovers)系列作品。

战后回到牛津攻读历史的她发现很难适应战后生活。结识了温妮弗莱德·霍尔特比,两人成为挚友,都渴望在伦敦文坛立足,遗憾的是霍尔特比1935年死于肾衰竭。布里坦的第一部小说《黑暗之潮》(The Dark Tide)因讽刺了牛津大学的教师,尤其是萨默维尔学院的教师,引发了丑闻。1933年,出版了成名作《青春誓言》(Testament of Youth)。1936年出版的小说《荣誉庄园》

（*Honourable Estate*）是一部自传体小说。自20世纪30年代以来，一直是和平主义杂志《和平新闻》的定期撰稿人，并最终成为该杂志编委。1944年，因在出版的《轰炸大屠杀》（*Massacre by Bombing*）一书中公开反对对德国城市轰炸而受到诽谤。后出版了《友谊誓言》（*Testament of Friendship*）、《经验的证明》（*Testament of Experience*）等作品。她的许多小说都是基于真实的人物和经历创作的。1981年，她将1913年到1917年的日记出版，名为《青春纪事》（*Chronicle of Youth*）。

也 许[①]

太阳会再次升起
我会再次看到蔚蓝的天
也许会再次感到生的欢喜
尽管没有了你

脚下是碧绿的草地
明媚的春光让人无比欢愉
也许洁白香甜的山楂花会再次让我欣喜
尽管你已离去

夏日的树叶闪着亮光
深红色的玫瑰再次绽放
秋收的田野一片欢畅
尽管你不在身旁

当悲苦的一年将尽
也许我会从痛苦中解脱
会再听一遍圣诞歌
尽管你已听不到

美好的时光会让欢乐再现
但最大的欢喜已与我无缘

失去你，我的心
早已碎了

注释

① 该诗献给未婚夫罗兰·奥布里·莱顿。他于1915年在诗人接受求婚4个月后被一名狙击手击毙，时年20岁。

回旋诗

（"重伤致死"）
你死了，我再无安宁之日
孤自穿梭于寂寥的世界
追梦已是徒劳
因为你死了

我将打发无聊短暂的时光
虽然生活还有不少值得去爱
但无法找回我的胜利和骄傲

幻灭逐渐
侵蚀掉一切
无论怎样努力，都不再有收获
因为你死了

1914年8月

上帝说,"人类已把我忘记:
沉睡的灵魂会再次觉醒
蒙蔽的双眼一定要会明鉴"

人类只能在痛苦中被救赎
因此上帝用惩罚的棍棒鞭挞地球上的人类
人间便遭受了可怕的毁灭

在上帝营造的荒芜和废墟里
饱受苦难的人们
在绝望中哭喊"根本没有上帝"

查尔斯·汉密尔顿·索利

（Charles Hamilton Sorley，1895—1915）

被认为是战争诗人萨松和欧文的先驱。

英国陆军军官和战争诗人。生于苏格兰阿伯丁，父亲威廉·里奇·索利是哲学家和大学教授。曾在剑桥大学国王学院、马尔堡学院接受教育。在马尔堡学院，他最喜欢的运动是雨中越野跑。之后到德国耶拿大学学习。第一次世界大战爆发后，自愿回国服军役。1915年8月，晋升为上尉。1915年10月在卢斯战役中阵亡。他的最后一首诗《当你看到数百万无嘴的死人》（*When You See Millions of the Mouthless Dead*）是阵亡后从他的工具包里找到的。《马尔堡及其他诗歌》（*Marlborough and Other Poems*）于1916年1月追授出版，当年就印刷了6个版本。《书信集》（*Collected Letters*）由其父母编辑，1919年出版。

他的去世被认为是诗歌界的巨大损失。罗伯特·格雷夫斯在《告别一切》（*Goodbye to All That*）一书中把他描述为"三位阵亡的重要诗人之一"（其他两位是罗森伯格和欧文）。索利被视为萨松和欧文的先驱。

1919年，查尔斯·伍德给他的诗作《期望》（*Expectans*

expectavi）的最后两节配乐，该颂歌很快就成为了圣公会大教堂和学院教堂的演奏曲目。1985年11月11日，在威斯敏斯特教堂的诗人角，揭幕了一块纪念第一次世界大战期间阵亡的16位诗人的纪念碑，索利是其中最年轻的一位。

这，这就是死亡

这，这就是死亡：没有胜利：没有失败：
只有一个空桶，一块擦净的石板
死亡仁慈地拾掇了一切

我们知道：死亡不是日渐衰竭的生命
是突然被碾碎的生命，是突然破裂的桶
历经世事的我们也不知其结局

征服者和被征服者在死亡这里无差异：
是懦夫还是勇士，朋友或敌人，鬼魂们不会追问：
"喂，你咽气的时候记录上写的什么？"

死亡将贫瘠、缺憾的往昔
隐去
当那早年的铮铮誓言被提起
它搅动、升腾、扩散，绽出花来，芬芳四溢
这就是死去的你

当你看到数百万无嘴的死人

当你在梦中看到数百万无嘴的死人
在苍白的阵营里走着
请记着：不要像旁人那样，讲温柔的话语
你不必
也无须赞美他们。他们已经聋了，怎能听到？
怎知道那堆砌在他们炸开的头颅上的赞美不是咒语？
也不要哭。他们失明的眼睛看不见你的泪
也无须授予他们荣誉。荣誉瞬间烟消云散
只说"他们死了。"再补充一句
"之前许多更优秀的也死了。"
然后，扫视那堆在一起的尸体，也许
你能察觉到一张曾爱过的脸
但现在已成幽灵。没有一张面孔你能认出
死亡已将一切据为己有

罗伯特·格雷夫斯（Robert Graves，1895—1985）

他的诗歌影响了英国桂冠诗人泰德·休斯和西尔维娅·普拉斯——继艾米莉·狄金森和伊丽莎白·毕肖普之后最重要的美国女诗人。

英国诗人、历史小说家、评论家，古拉丁语和古希腊语的杰出翻译家，一生创作了140多部作品。

生于温布尔登的中产阶级家庭，其父是参与了爱尔兰复兴运动的爱尔兰诗人阿尔弗雷德·珀西瓦尔·格雷夫斯。1913年，获得牛津大学圣约翰学院的奖学金，到牛津大学接受教育。

1914年第一次世界大战爆发后应征入伍，1915年10月26日被提升为上尉。1916年，出版了第一本诗集《火盆之上》（*Over the Brazier*），主要记录了前线的经历，他也因此被誉为现实主义诗人。在索姆河战役中受伤，与同团的著名战争诗人西格弗里德·萨松一同在牛津大学的萨默维尔学院接受康复治疗。格雷夫斯将自己和萨松之间的友谊记录在信件和传记中，他们的故事被帕特·巴克在小说《再生》中呈现，该小说已被改编为同名电影。

一战结束后，22岁的他与18岁的南希·尼科尔森喜结连理。1919年10月，进入牛津大学工作，期间与托马斯·爱德华·劳伦斯成为好友。1927年出版了传记《劳伦斯与阿拉伯人》(*Lawrence and the Arabs*),该书在商业上取得巨大成功。1929年出版自传《告别一切》(*Good-Bye to All That*),反响同样很好。他因关于罗马帝国的历史小说而出名。1934年,出版了最成功的商业著作《我,克劳迪斯》(*I, Claudius*),之后又出版了续集《克劳迪斯神》(*Claudius the God*)。有关克劳迪斯的书籍很快被改编成广受欢迎的电视连续剧。他也因这两部作品被授予詹姆斯·泰特·布莱克纪念奖。

1946年,出版了历史小说《耶稣王》(*King Jesus*)。1948年出版了对诗性的思辨研究著作《白色女神》(*The White Goddess*)后,转向科幻小说,创作了《新克里特岛的七天》(*Seven Days in New Crete*)等。1967年,与奥马尔·阿里·沙阿共同出版了奥马尔·海亚姆的《鲁拜亚特》(*Rubaiyat*)新译本。他的《十二个恺撒》(*The Twelve Caesars*)和《金驴》(*The Golden Ass*)的译本颇受欢迎。

死去的波奇

对于读过我的战争诗歌
和仅听过关于鲜血和荣誉的你们
我要说(或许您早已听过)
"战争是地狱!"如果你们和曾经的我一样怀疑
那么今天,在马梅茨伍德我找到了
对嗜血者的治愈:
我瞧见倚在破碎行李箱上的波奇
死在一堆血糊糊的污秽里
他的前方芳草萋萋
衣物上散发着恶臭,留着短发的他满脸痛苦
戴着眼镜的他大肚子裸露着
污黑的血顺着鼻子和胡须往下滴

塞西尔·戴·刘易斯
（Cecil Day-Lewis，1904—1972）

20世纪最伟大的诗人之一。英国桂冠诗人。

爱尔兰诗人、英国皇家文学会副主席、美国文学艺术学会荣誉会员，被认为是20世纪最伟大的诗人之一。是著名演员、奥斯卡奖得主丹尼尔·戴·刘易斯和纪录片导演塔玛辛·戴·刘易斯的父亲。刘易斯在牛津求学时认识了W.H.奥登，写作风格受其影响，奥登还帮他校订了《牛津诗集》（*Oxford Poetry*）。1925年出版了第一部诗集《山毛榉守夜及其他诗作》（*Beechen Vigil and Other Poems*）。1929年，代表作《过渡诗集》（*Transitional Poem*）确立了他抒情诗人的地位。二战期间，在英国情报部担任出版主编，此时已摆脱奥登的影响，这一时期的代表作有《全世界》（*World Over All*）。1946年成为剑桥大学的一名讲师，并将自己的演讲整理成书——《诗歌意象》（*The Poetic Image*）。1951年至1956年间，在牛津大学讲授诗歌，1962年至1963年任哈佛大学诺顿教授。1968年继约翰·梅斯菲尔德之后获得"桂冠诗人"头衔。除了诗歌，他还以笔名尼古拉斯·布莱克发表了多部侦探小说，代表作有《内有泄底》（*A Question of Proof*）、《你，死亡之壳》（*Thou Shell of*

Death)、《这个人必须死》(*The Man Must Die*),《这个畜生必须死》(*The Beast Must Die*)和《要有麻烦了》(*There's Trouble Brewing*)等。因生前崇拜托马斯·哈代,去世后被安葬在英国多塞特圣米迦勒教堂哈代墓地旁边。

志愿军[1]

告诉在英格兰的他们,倘若他们问
是什么让我们参战
让我们来到这高原
在这繁星下的墓地长眠

不是愚昧、不是欺骗
也不为荣耀、复仇或报酬
我们来这里是因为我们睁着的眼
看不到别的出路

再没有别的路可以让
人类摇曳的真理之光永放光芒
头顶的星光可以作证:我们的人生
固然短暂,但绝不暗淡

越过这片废弃的橄榄林
那边最远处的高地
曾是我们的领土
为了重新拥有它,我们来到此处

照耀我们吧,记忆中和现实里
那绿水环绕的绸缎般的牧场

家乡的河流,请用你的力量
刷新我们前进的路

在这片陌生的焦土上
我们为自由的英格兰而战
我们伟大的祖先希望看到
他们曾为英格兰赢得的土地

注释

① 诗歌标题"志愿军"和诗歌里的发声者是投身西班牙内战（1936—1939）的国际纵队里的英国志愿者。该诗是献给国际纵队的颂歌。

约翰·贝杰曼（John Betjeman，1906—1984）

英国桂冠诗人，以幽默诗见长。

英国诗人、作家、播音员。生于英国伦敦，家中独子。1925年进入牛津大学莫德林学院学习，未能获得学位。离开牛津后，结识了诗人路易斯·麦克尼斯和W.H.奥登，两位诗人对其之后的创作产生了一定影响。1930年成为《建筑评论》的助理编辑。

两年后第一本诗集《锡安山》（*Mount Zion*）由好友爱德华·詹姆斯出版。1937年出版了第二本诗集《不竭的露水》（*Continual Dew*）。从20世纪30年代到70年代，相继出版多部诗集：《新圣坛的古老之光》（*Old Lights For New Chancels*）、《古钟楼内的新蝙蝠》（*New Bats in Old Belfries*）、《迟开的菊花》（*A Few Late Chrysanthemums*）、《门廊里的诗歌》（*Poems in the Porch*）、《被钟声唤起》（*Summoned by Bells*）、《高和低》（*High and Low*）以及1974年出版的最后一部诗集《寒气逼人》（*A Nip in the Air*）。其诗歌幽默风趣。1969年荣获"桂冠诗人"头衔。

泥　沼

来吧，亲爱的炸弹，请落在这片泥沼里
这儿已不适合人类
这里寸草不生，一头牛都供养不起
死亡，请来占领吧

来吧，炸弹
把这配有空调的明亮食堂
这罐装的水果、肉、牛奶和豆子
这被禁锢的思想、呼吸都炸成碎片

把他们称作城镇的那个烂摊子搅乱
这所九十七年的房子
二十年来
以一星期一个半克朗[①]维护着

击中这个总是欺骗总是获胜的
双下巴男人
他总是用女人的泪水
洗濯他肮脏的肌肤

来吧，炸碎他那发亮的橡木桌
炸碎他那双时常中风的手

不让他再讲那无聊肮脏的笑话
让他歇斯底里地咆哮吧

请饶了那些光头职员
他们只是那个臭男人的跟班
他们疯了,但这不是他们的错
他们已将地狱体验过

他们听不懂收音机里的鸟鸣
这不能怪他们
他们经常去梅登黑德②
这也不是他们的错

在冒牌的都铎酒吧
他们谈论着汽车品牌和体育赛事
他们只是打打嗝
从没敢仰望过星空

在他们雇不起帮工的家
妻子们小心地卷着自己灰白的头发
一边在浑浊的空气里晾干头发
一边涂染指甲

来吧,友好的炸弹,请落在泥沼里

为这些已经备好的犁

卷心菜就要露头

大地开始呼吸

注释

① 克朗：瑞典的货币单位。1克朗约等于0.68元人民币。

② 梅登黑德：英格兰伯克郡的一个贸易繁荣的小镇。

在威斯敏斯特教堂

人声鼎沸
我要将另一只手套脱去
美丽的伊甸园
此刻正沐浴在威斯敏斯特教堂的钟声里
在这英格兰政要的长眠之地
请聆听一位女士的哭泣

仁慈的主啊,请把炸弹投向德国
以您的仁爱,请宽恕他们的女人
倘若不便
我们会原谅您的失误
不过,仁爱的主,无论如何
切莫让任何人炸我

请保佑我们的帝国永不分裂
用您的圣手指引我们的兵力
那来自遥远的牙买加、洪都拉斯
和多哥等国的英勇的黑人兄弟
请在战争中保护他们
特别要保护我们白人

想想我们的国家代表着什么

博姿店里的书籍 乡间小路
言论自由，航道畅通，社会等级分明
广泛的民主和完善的下水道
主啊，请您特别关照
卡多根广场①189号

亲爱的主，即使我有罪
但并未违法乱纪
只要有空
我定会做晚祷
所以，主啊，为了我的钱
请不要让我的股票下跌

为了您的王国，我会辛勤劳作
助我们的战士赢得胜利
给懦夫们送去白羽毛②
我会加入妇女陆战团
然后在绝对安全的地域
把您宝座四周的台阶清洗

现在我觉得好多了
能在这里——
杰出政要的长眠之地
聆听您的教诲是多么不易

主啊，恕我先走一步
我还有一个午宴要赴

注释

① 卡多根广场：又被称为卡多根花园，是伦敦骑士桥地带的一个居民广场，以卡多根伯爵的名字命名。
② 18世纪起，白羽毛在英国是懦弱、胆小的象征，被爱国者群体用来羞辱不愿意参军的人。

W.H.奥登（Wystan Hugh Auden，1907—1973）

凭借长诗《焦虑时代》获得普利策诗歌奖。他拥有"20世纪最伟大的思想"。

英国诗人，评论家，举世公认的20世纪最伟大的作家之一。诗歌界最具影响力的人物之一。创作了400多首风格各异的诗歌，还创作了戏剧、散文、剧本、游记和评论作品。

生于英国约克郡，在伯明翰附近的一个中产阶级家庭中长大。父亲是医生，母亲是传教士、护士，其家庭是坚定的英国天主教徒，早年生活为他一生从事科学、心理分析和基督教研究奠定了基础。从寄宿学校毕业后，因获得牛津大学生物学奖学金，在牛津大学基督教堂学院学习生物，后改学英语。从老师J.R.R·托尔金那里学习了古英语诗歌。与斯蒂芬·斯彭德、塞西尔·戴·刘易斯和路易斯·麦克尼斯等左翼诗人缔结了深厚的友谊。1930年第一本书《诗歌》（Poems）引起广泛关注，1932年出版了《演说家》（The Orators）。20世纪30年代战争的阴云逐渐笼罩，他被视为那一代人的主要代言人。1939年1月，离开英国前往纽约，同行的还有克里斯托弗·伊舍伍德，后者是他的文学导师、合作者和情人。后与一位年轻的美国诗人切斯特·卡尔曼相识、相知，后者成为他一生的伴侣。1947年，凭借长诗《焦虑时代》（*The Age of Anxiety*）获得普利策诗歌奖，该诗的标题成为描述现代处境的流行短语。1956年至1961年，他担任牛津大学诗歌教授，讲座深受学生和教职员工的欢迎，并成为1962年出版的散文集《染工之手》（*The Dyer's Hand*）的基础。1973年逝于维也纳。

  奥登是一位多产的作家，其作品涉及文学、政治、心理和宗教等主题。他的诗歌运用了所有可以想象到的诗节模式，从民谣到俳句、十四行诗和维拉内拉诗，从短抒情诗到长篇冥想。他是文体形式方面的大师，寻求以不同的方式来理解个人、社会和人类总体状况的关系。最著名的关于爱情的诗歌有《葬礼蓝调》（*Funeral Blues*）等；关于政治和社会主题的诗歌有《1939年9月1日》（*The Shield of Achilles September 1, 1939*）和《阿喀琉斯之盾》（*The Shield of Achilles*）等；关于文化和心理主题的诗歌有《焦虑时代》等；关于宗教主题的诗歌有《暂时》（*For The Time Being*）和《祈祷时刻》（*Horae Canonicae*）等。他还参与纪录片、诗剧等各类表演。整个职业生涯中，他既饱受争议又颇具影响力。

无名士兵墓志铭

为了拯救你的世界,你让此人去死
如果现在见到你,他可会当面质问你——为什么?

阿喀琉斯之盾①

她②的目光越过他③的肩头
寻找葡萄藤、橄榄树
治理井然的大理石城市
和波涛汹涌的海面上的船舰
但在那闪亮的金盾上
他的双手锻造出的却是
一片人为的荒地
和铅灰的天宇

单调、光秃秃的棕色平原
无一片草叶,无生活气息
无食物可充饥,无处可栖
但就在这荒漠地
却聚集着数量惊人的人们
百万只眼睛,百万双靴子列队伫立
面无表情,等待着一个手势

不知从哪飘来这样一个声音
统计数据证明,某些事业是正义的
那语调和此荒漠地一样单调、枯燥
无人欢呼,无人商榷
一队接一队,在扬起的尘土里

他们齐步行进,坚信
他们定在某处罹难

她的目光越过他的肩头
寻找仪式上的虔敬:
戴着白色花冠的牛犊
酒水和别的祭品
但见他摇曳的炉火旁
那闪亮的金盾上
那本该是祭坛的地方
却是另一番景象

装有倒刺的铁丝网围住了专权之地
百无聊赖的官员们懒散地躺在那里(一位在说笑)
天气酷热,哨兵们汗流浃背
一群正义的民众往里观望
当面色苍白的三个人被押出来
绑在地上的三个笔直的木桩上
他们没挪步,也没吱声

这世上无论民众还是帝王
都不可估量,都富有影响
但当被掌握在别人手上;就没了分量
别指望帮忙,也无人肯帮;

当敌人屡屡得逞
他们的羞耻无以复加;没了自尊
在肉体死亡之前先失去了为人

她的目光越过他的肩头
寻找竞技场里中的选手
寻找随着音乐的快节奏
四肢快速舞动的
陶醉的男男女女
但见那闪亮的盾牌上
他双手锻造的不是舞厅
而是衰草遍地的荒漠

一个弃儿身着破衫
在荒原上踽踽独行
一只鸟儿躲过了他投掷的石子:
两个姑娘遭强奸,两个少年杀了另一少年
这都是他亲眼所见
他从未听说世界会信守诺言
也未听见人们因他人哭泣而呜咽

兵器锻造大师——薄嘴唇的赫菲斯托斯
一瘸一拐地走了
胸膛发亮的忒提斯——

绝望地哭喊
怨恨上帝纵容她的儿子——
力大无比的阿喀琉斯
铁石心肠的他残忍地杀人
末了也在劫难逃

注释

① 诗歌标题源自奥登获得美国国家图书奖的同名诗集，表达了奥登的政治观点。借荷马史诗中火神赫菲斯托斯为阿喀琉斯锻造盾牌一事，对当代文明进行尖锐的批评。在特洛伊战争中英雄阿喀琉斯将自己的盾牌借给好友帕特洛克罗斯。特洛伊英雄、大王子赫克托耳在太阳神阿波罗的暗中帮助下，杀死了帕特洛克罗斯，并夺走了盾牌。阿喀琉斯悲痛万分，决心为好友报仇，与赫克托耳决一死战。为此，他的母亲忒提斯特地请火神赫菲斯托斯为她儿子再锻造一面新盾。在这面新盾上火神刻下大地、海洋、日月星辰，还有一座和平安宁的城池和一座正被战火毁坏的城池。荷马描述的盾牌上欣欣向荣的场景在奥登笔下成了迥异的噩梦般的战争场景。
② 她：即下文的忒提斯。（参阅P145注释10）
③ 他：即下文的火神赫菲斯托斯，对应罗马神话中的伏尔甘。根据《荷马史诗》，赫菲斯托斯是宙斯与赫拉的儿子（另一版本是赫拉靠自己的意志力独自将其诞下）。由于赫菲斯托斯长相丑陋，被赫拉丢弃于奥林匹斯山下，赫菲斯托斯在空中翻腾了一天，落到利姆诺斯岛上，从此摔成了瘸

子。幸运的是，他被海洋女神忒提斯捡到并收养。长大后，他学会了各种手艺，技艺高超，被誉为工匠的始祖及锻造的庇护神。

克利福德·戴门特
（Clifford Dyment，1914—1971）

曾在 BBC 广播电台和电视台担任播音员。

英国诗人、文学评论家、编辑和记者，以撰写乡村题材的诗歌闻名。

出生于德比郡的阿尔弗里顿，父母是威尔士人。参加第一次世界大战的父亲在他4岁时阵亡于法国亚眠。在乌斯克河畔，卡利恩度过了童年，他在莱斯特郡的拉夫堡文法学校接受教育，后迁到伦敦，开启写作生涯。1935年出版第一本诗集《第一天》（*First Day*）。20世纪30年代，已成为伦敦文学界的知名人物。1937年一个偶然的机会，他发现了应征入伍的父亲阵亡前写的一封信而创作了诗歌《儿子》（*The Son*）。

此外，他从事新闻和文学批评工作。第二次世界大战期间，为英国政府工作，从事电影制作。1950年获得了洛克菲勒基金会大西洋奖。1971年，菲利普·拉金将他的诗作《作为一个有着丰富需求的男孩，我漫游》（*As a Boy with a Richness of Needs I Wandered*）收录在《牛津20世纪英语诗集》中。曾在BBC广播电台和电视台担任播音员。1971年逝于伦敦。

贝蒂·罗为他的诗歌《老鼠》（*Mouse*）配乐，将其作为她的歌曲《猫和老鼠》的一部分。

儿　子

在一个纸箱里,我发现这封信,一段尘封的历史
展开这封深藏了多年的信
信纸干皱
黑色的字迹已褪为棕色
信是一个前线士兵写的——
表达他的爱,和他未实现的愿望——他想离开前线
这句被划掉了。末了,他写道:
我的运气坠入海底

窗外阳光普照,世界一片光亮
我听着收音机,有人在大笑
我没有唱,没有笑,也没有欣赏阳光
在这安静的房间,我想起他
我阵亡的父亲和其他阵亡的人们
他们的运气坠入海底

狄兰·托马斯（Dylan Thomas，1914—1953）

狄兰·托马斯是苹果公司创始人斯蒂芬·乔布斯最喜欢的诗人。电影《星际穿越》引用了他的诗歌《不要温顺地走进那良宵》。

英国当代作家，天才传奇人物。20世纪30年代英美诗坛杰出的诗人，其非凡的诗艺掀开了英美诗歌史上的新篇章。

出生于英国南威尔士的斯旺西。早期在父亲执教的斯旺西文法中学学习，并开始诗歌创作。他自诩为"库姆唐金大道的兰波"。1933年在伦敦《新英格兰周刊》首次发表诗作，1934年获"诗人之角"图书奖。随后出版诗集《诗18首》（18 Poems）、《诗25首》（25 Poems）、《爱的地图》（The Map of Love）等。二战时，担任英国BBC广播公司播音员，用他富有音乐性和感染力的演说征服了千百万听众。

一个有着自我毁灭激情的浪漫主义诗人，一个天生的顽童，而后又成为酒鬼、烟鬼，人们口中"疯狂的狄兰"。多次访美，并以其狂放的、抑扬顿挫的、极富感染力的朗诵在美国引起轰动。在他最后一次访美时误用大量吗啡，致昏迷，卒于纽约，年仅39岁。而他点石成金的语言魔力至今仍吸引、启发着后人，"生、欲、死"等主题的诗歌影响了几代欧美人。

1882年，在英国伦敦威斯敏斯特大教堂的诗人角，纪念狄兰·托马斯的墓碑揭幕，上面刻着他的名诗《羊齿山》（*Fern Hill*）里的诗句："纵使时光掌控我的青翠和死亡/枷锁中的我也要像大海般自由地歌唱。"2014年，在他诞辰100周年之际，英国皇家造币厂发行了一枚他半身塑像的纪念币。纪念币上羊齿叶的设计也是因其名作《羊齿山》。

那只签署文件的手

那只签署文件的手毁了一座城
五根掌权的手指扼杀了生机
国家分裂，尸横遍野
五根不可一世的手指置一位君王于死地

伛偻的身躯探出那只威重令行的手
指关节僵硬、痉挛
鹅毛笔一挥——结束会谈
终结杀戮

那只签约的手带来瘟疫
饥荒蔓延，蝗灾四起
那只以潦草签名掌控大众命运的手
真是奇迹

五根不可一世的手指清点着亡者
却未抚慰创伤，安抚悲秋
一手压制情感，一手掌控天国
权高位重的手怎有悲悯与情柔

伊芙·梅里亚姆（Eve Merriam，1916—1992）

1982年百老汇音乐剧《街头之梦》基于她的作品《内城鹅妈妈》。

美国诗人和剧作家。出生于宾夕法尼亚的费城，先后在康奈尔大学、宾夕法尼亚大学、威斯康星大学和哥伦比亚大学接受教育。梅里亚姆的第一本书《家庭圈》（*Family Circle*）获得了耶鲁大学青年诗人奖。

她的童谣集《内城鹅妈妈》（*The Inner City Mother Goose*）曾被列为禁书。1971年百老汇音乐剧《内城》的灵感源于此书，后在1982年以《街头之梦》重新上演。1956年出版了《艾玛·拉扎勒斯：拿着火把的女人》（*Emma Lazarus: Woman with a Torch*）。她不仅为成人创作，还是一位儿童作家，先后出版了30多本书，1981年她荣获NCTE儿童诗歌优秀奖。

戏剧《走出父亲的房子》改编于她的《在美国长大的女性》（*Growing Up Female in America*），于1978年在《伟大的表演》系列节目中播出。

懦　夫

你在战场中大哭，我和你一起哭
你想悄然逃离
靠近点，我们一起逃离此地
我也内疚、羞愧
逃兵朋友，我绝不举报你
我是你颤抖的孪生兄弟！
我们都恐惧，我们的双膝因恐惧战栗
从枪口下逃离，我们竟不期而遇
躲在我战栗的大腿下：我就是你妈妈
虽然只有我们俩
但我们的哀嚎直抵世界的尽头
吓坏了，我的患难兄弟
吓坏了，我们委实吓坏了
必须有人坦露心迹
懦夫须挽懦夫的手

约翰·列侬（John Lennon，1940—1980）

作为披头士乐队的创始成员闻名全球。在BBC"最伟大的100名英国人"榜单中被民众票选为第八位。

英国歌手和词曲作者，他作为披头士乐队的创始成员闻名全球。英国最高骑士勋章（Most Excellent Order of the British Empire，简称MBE）的拥有者。该乐队是流行音乐史上最具影响力的乐队。在1999年英国举行的全国诗歌日上，BBC宣布"英国人最爱的歌词"的投票结果是列侬的《想象》（*Imagine*）。

生于利物浦，没有通过任何一门普通教育证书（O-level）考试。在姨妈和校长的努力下被利物浦艺术学院录取，后因扰乱课堂被开除。青少年时期投身噪音爵士乐热潮，1960年，他的第一支乐队采石工人改名为披头士乐团。1962年，与辛西娅结婚。1963年初，披头士在英国取得了商业成功，长子朱利安同年4月出生。1968年结识日本先锋派女艺术家小野洋子，1969年再婚，并在自己的名字上加了"小野"。1970年披头士解散后，他开始发展个人职业生涯，发行了颇受好评的专辑《塑胶小野乐队》（*Plastic Ono Band*）以及标志性的歌曲《想象》、《工人阶级英雄》（*Working Class Hero*）等。他在音乐、写作、绘画、影片和采访中展现了反叛的天性和辛辣的幽默。他的一些歌曲诸如《想象》、《给和平一个机会》（*Give Peace a Chance*）等被视为反战歌曲。对越战的批评使尼克松政府试图把他驱逐出境。1975年，从乐坛隐退，在纽约家中照顾他和小野洋子的幼子西恩。1980年，携新专辑《双重幻想》（*Double Fantasy*）复出，在专辑发行3周后被一歌迷枪杀。

　　2002年，在BBC的"最伟大的100名英国人"榜单中被民众票选为第八位。2002年，利物浦的机场被重命名为利物浦约翰·列侬机场。2008年，《滚石》杂志把他选为"史上最伟大的歌手"第五位。2013年12月，国际天文联合会将水星上的一个陨石坑以列侬命名。2018年9月7日，美国纽约邮政局发行了一枚印有列侬照片的邮票。音乐历史学家尤里什和比伦来认为列侬最重要的贡献是"创作出了为人类处境、描述人类处境、面向人类处境自我剖析的歌曲"。

想　象

想象没有天堂
如果你愿意，这不费吹灰之力
想象我们的下面没有地狱
头顶只是辽阔的天宇
想象这世上的人们，都享受着当下……

想象没有国家
这不费什么力气
不去消灭谁，也不为谁就义
也没有宗教分歧
所有的人们，都生活在和平里……

你可能会说我在呓语
但我并非唯一
希望有一天你能与我们在一起
天下归一

想象没有什么疆土领地
不知你是否可以
没有贪婪或碌碌饥肠
四海皆兄弟
所有的人们，一同享受这世界的美丽……

你可能会说我在呓语

但我并非唯一

希望有一天你能与我们在一起

天下归一

给和平一个机会

人人都在谈论
套袋主义，杂乱主义，拖沓主义，癫狂主义，邋遢主义，
　　肮脏主义①
这主义，那主义，主义主义主义？

我们只想说 给和平一个机会
我们只想说 给和平一个机会

人人都在谈论
部长高管，恶人坏蛋，楼梯扶栏，瓶瓶罐罐
主教，鱼贩，学者专家和他们的大突眼
还有再见，还有睡眠

我们只想说 给和平一个机会
我们只想说 给和平一个机会

让我来告知你
人人都在谈论
革命论，演变论，粉碎论
鞭笞论，管理论，融合论
冥想论，联合国论，恭贺论

我们只想说 给和平一个机会

我们只想说 给和平一个机会

人人都在谈论

约翰[2]、洋子[3]、蒂米·利里[4]、露丝玛丽[5]、汤米·斯莫瑟斯[6]、鲍勃·迪伦[7]

汤米·库珀[8]、德勒克·泰勒[9]、诺曼·梅勒[10]

艾伦·金斯伯格[11]、哈瑞·奎师那[12]

哈瑞、哈瑞·奎师那

我们只想说 给和平一个机会吧

我们只想说 给和平一个机会吧

我们只想说 给和平一个机会吧

我们只想说 给和平一个机会吧

……

注释

[1] 原文中这一行的英语单词都是词作者列侬根据需要在词根上添加ism杜撰出来的,讽刺那些无关紧要的理论主义或派别。

[2] 约翰:约翰·列侬本人。

[3] 洋子(1933—):即小野洋子,列侬的第二任妻子和遗孀。日裔美籍多媒体艺术家、歌手及和平活动家。以其先锋派艺术、音乐和电影领域的作品而知名。

[4] 蒂米·利里(1920—1996):美国心理学家和作家,以大

力倡导迷幻药物而闻名。20世纪六七十年代，被捕36次。尼克松总统称他为"美国最危险的人"。

⑤露丝玛丽（1935—2002）：美国女演员。代表作《打开、收听、退出》。与上文的蒂米·利里是夫妻。

⑥汤米·斯莫瑟斯（1937—2023）美国喜剧演员、作曲家、音乐家。和弟弟迪克组成喜剧二人组。

⑦鲍勃·迪伦（1941—）：美国民谣及摇滚歌手、诗人、画家，在国内最著名的歌曲是《答案在风中飘扬》《暴雨将至》。2016年荣获诺贝尔文学奖。

⑧汤米·库珀（1921—1984）：威尔士喜剧演员和魔术师。

⑨德勒克·泰勒（1932—1997）：英国记者、作家、公关人员和唱片制作人。曾是甲壳虫乐队的新闻发布人。

⑩诺曼·梅勒（1923—2007）：美国小说家和记者。因使用一种新的新闻形式而闻名，该形式结合了文学富有想象力的主观性和新闻业的客观性。

⑪艾伦·金斯伯格（1926—1997）：美国诗人，"垮掉派"的灵魂人物。代表作《嚎叫》。

⑫哈瑞·奎师那：基于古印度吠陀的大型印度教宗教团体奎师那派及奎师那派教徒，也是国际奎师那意识协会的简称。该协会认为人并非躯体，而是灵魂。主张和平、素食主义、一夫一妻制。

大卫·克里格（David Krieger，1942—2023）

核时代和平基金会的创始人。

心理学家、和平运动的领导人和诗人。核时代和平基金会（NAPF）的创始人，自1982年以来一直担任该基金会的主席，并加入了多个反战和支持裁军的组织。

出生于美国洛杉矶，后举家定居西雅图。父亲是儿科医生。以心理学学士学位毕业于西方学院，后拥有夏威夷大学政治学硕士和博士学位以及圣巴巴拉法学院的法学博士学位。早期在夏威夷大学和旧金山州立大学任助理教授。曾担任圣巴巴拉高等法院的法官。曾在日本广岛做博士研究，在那里的所见所闻使他决心以毕生的力量为废除核武器、维护世界和平贡献自己的力量。

在各个领域均有建树，荣誉颇丰。2000年获得《国际人文与和平杂志》和平奖，分别在2005年、2007年、2010年荣获诸多诗歌大奖。经常参加讨论裁军问题的电视和广播节目。著有许多关于核时代和平的书籍，其中包括：《和平100种思想》（*Peace 100 Ideas*）、《黑暗时代的希望：对人类未来的反思》（*Hope in a Dark Time: Reflections on Humanity's Future*）、《和平的诗意》（*The Poetry of Peace*）、《选择希望：在核时代的你对缔造和平的作用》

(*Choose Hope:Your Role in Waging Peace in the Nuclear Age*)等。

撰写了数百篇文章,发表在《洛杉矶时报》《基督教科学箴言报》《真相》《共同梦想》和《反击》等报纸上。所写的文章《创造一个没有核武器的世界》(*Creating a World without Nuclear Weapons*)被收录在《一个国家的梦想:如何让美国变得更好》一书中。

大卫·克里格一生致力于维护世界和平,连续10年被提名诺贝尔和平奖。

伊拉克孩子有姓名[①]

伊拉克孩子有姓名
他们并非无名无姓

伊拉克孩子有面孔
他们并非无颜孩童

伊拉克孩子并非长着萨达姆的模样
他们拥有自己可爱的脸庞

伊拉克孩子有自己的姓名
他们并不全叫萨达姆·侯赛因

伊拉克孩子有心灵
他们并非无心无肺

伊拉克孩子有梦想
他们并非没有愿望

伊拉克孩子有心跳
他们不只是战争中的数字

伊拉克孩子有笑容

他们并非死气沉沉

伊拉克孩子双眸闪亮
他们敏捷、活跃，笑声朗朗

伊拉克孩子满怀憧憬
他们并非没有理想

伊拉克孩子也会害怕
他们并非无所畏惧

伊拉克孩子有姓名
他们不叫意外死伤

该如何称呼他们？
称他们奥马尔，穆罕默德，法赫德

称他们马尔瓦和蒂巴
请叫他们的名字吧

请不要视之为战争数据
更不要称之为意外死伤

注释

① 这首诗是作者于伊拉克战争前夕写的,在2002年底和2003年初的众多和平游行中被宣读。当时,世界各地的许多人走上街头,希望阻止战争的发生。

比战争更糟糕的[①]

比战争,比那无休止的、无意义的战争更糟糕的
比引发战争的谎言更糟糕的

比数不尽的伤亡更糟糕的
比藏起棺木和不参加葬礼更糟糕的

比蔑视国际法更糟糕的
比阿布格莱布监狱里的酷刑更糟糕的

比年轻士兵的堕落更糟糕的
比破坏集体道德感更糟糕的

比傲慢无礼、洋洋自得、趾高气扬更糟糕的
比诚信尽失更糟糕的
比失去自由更糟糕的

比不以史为鉴更糟糕的
比毁掉未来更糟糕的
比极度的愚蠢更糟糕的

比以上种种都更糟糕的
是沉默,是美国多数民众的沉默

仿佛一场战争、一个国家或一生还不够糟糕

注释

① 这首诗创作于2004年6月,此时伊拉克战争已开战1年多。诗中,作者思考了一系列比战争更糟糕的事情。

致一名伊拉克男孩——阿里·伊斯梅尔·阿巴斯[①]

你想当医生?

你的梦想
难以实现了

我们的炮弹不是冲着你的

它们本是智能炮弹,但是它们不知道
你想当医生

它们不了解你
对爱也一无所知

不能给予它们幻想

它们只知发现目标
完成爆炸任务

它们只是锻造的有暴力内核的灰色金属壳
完成既定任务

找上你不是它们的错

或许你注定当不了医生

注释

① 这首诗写于2005年4月，是关于一个12岁的男孩阿里·伊斯梅尔·阿巴斯的故事。他的双亲、兄弟及其他11个亲戚都在美国导弹击中他家时丧生。男孩曾梦想当一名医生，但这次袭击使他失去双臂。

在巴格达问候布什①

"这是诀别之吻,狗东西。"
——蒙塔德尔·扎伊迪②

你是我国的不速之客
当然,不速之客也是客

你站在我们面前等候赞誉
我们岂能赞美你?

你们的战机毁了我们的家园
接着,你来了

你们的士兵冲进我们家门
侮辱男性,欺凌妇女

我们不是荒蛮小镇
你更不是我们的头领

你们是施虐者
我们知道你们给战俘强行灌水

我们见过战俘赤裸的身体

被你们狂吠的恶犬威逼

你，最不招待见的客人
你造成了更多的孤儿寡妻

我将我的左鞋③
扔向你一脸的痴笑
右鞋，摔向你满脸的无耻
我唯以此赠你

注释

① 这首诗创作于2008年12月，战争即将结束之际，以乔治·布什访问伊拉克并在那里对媒体发表讲话时发生的扔鞋子事件为蓝本。

② 蒙塔德尔·扎伊迪：伊拉克独立电视台巴格达迪亚的记者。扎伊迪扔鞋事件在伊拉克掀起了轩然大波。

③ 因为鞋子被踩在地上，且脏兮兮的，在伊拉克，用鞋子打人被认为是对人最大的侮辱。

扎伊德的不幸[①]

扎伊德不幸
生于伊拉克,这个国家
盛产石油

伊拉克不幸
遭他国入侵,这个入侵国
贪图石油

贪图石油的国家不幸
被人误导,这个人[②]
渴望战争

扎伊德的不幸升级
当他父母在自家诊所前
被射杀

他最大的不幸是
年仅11岁的他
父母双亡

在扎伊德的不幸中
长久的沉默

吞没了战争的喧嚣

注释

① 这首诗写于2010年7月,是一首关于伊拉克孩子的诗。
② 指乔治·布什,他以反恐的名义发动伊拉克战争,企图以此来获得美国人民对伊拉克战争的支持。

安德鲁·莫伸（Andrew Motion，1952— ）

自他伊始，桂冠诗人不再是终身制，改为10年一届。

英国诗人、小说家及传记作者。1952年生于伦敦，毕业于牛津大学。先后担任编辑、教授等职，是皇家文学学会会员。1977年出版诗集《快乐轮船》（*The Pleasure Steamers*）；1984年出版诗集《危险游戏：诗歌1974—1984》（*Dangerous Play: Poems，1974—1984*），该诗集获莱斯文学奖。1987年出版的叙事诗《自然原因》（*Natural Causes*）获狄兰·托马斯文学奖。在赫尔大学任教期间，莫伸与大学图书管理员同时是诗人的菲利普·拉金成为挚友。拉金逝世后，他亲自撰写传记《菲利普·拉金：一位作家的人生》（*Philip Larkin: A Writer's Life*）。该传记荣获惠特布莱德传记奖。还著有《约翰·济慈传》（*John Keats*），并创作了自传体散文。其小说作品包括《蛋糕博士的发明》（*The Invention of Dr.Cake*）、《银：重返金银岛》（*Silver: Return to Treasure Island*）和《新世界》（*The New World*）等。

1999年，莫伸继泰德·休斯之后成为"桂冠诗人"。他自愿打破桂冠诗人头衔的终身制，仅担任10年的桂冠诗人。在荣任桂冠诗人的10年（1999—2009）中，他破除传统，写了许多关于日常生活和大事件及皇室活动的诗歌。他还建立了诗歌档案馆。2009年，被封为爵士。

哈里·帕奇[①]之死

终于捱到次日拂晓

年轻的上尉爬向射击台

磕掉烟斗的烟灰,把热着的烟斗

塞进口袋,看了看手表

将哨子抿在唇齿间

6点钟他准时吹哨

但是今天,接下来的一切并未按原计划发生

悠扬的哨声

在这片废墟上回荡

躺着的成千上万的尸体

立刻站起。列队之际

他们像从前一样先把皮带勒紧

然后肩并肩,目视前方

为了加入这最后的招募,他们都离开长眠之地:

已经111岁的哈里·帕奇此刻也

迅速地踏着垫路板跑来

他就位后,整个方阵

整装待发,随军神父突然冒出

在每个人面前伫立片刻,而他们每人

都将粘在舌头上的干泥巴吐出

注释

① 哈里·帕奇：即哈里·约翰·帕奇（1898—2009），是大不列颠的超级世纪老人。他因为参加了第一次世界大战西线无人区的战役而广为人知，是第一次世界大战幸存士兵里活得最久的。

政权更迭[①]

死神沿着大路从尼尼微[②]启程
稍停片刻,说:"注意听,

"你们可看见周围那些地名?
如今它们都属于我,我已把它们翻了个底朝天

"占领伊甸,一路向南:
今日拂晓我命令军队拆了伊甸的城门和城垣

"让胜利就像树上的果子
人人看得见

"你们不是想吃吗?去,去吃吧
润一下唇,继续采折

"占领底格里斯河和幼发拉底河
它们曾从童年的画着阳光和沙滩的彩色石板上流过

"今非昔比,我已经用数不清的垃圾粪便
把它们填满

"占领巴比伦,那鲜花盛开的宫殿

和平年代里，花的芬芳在帝国的空气里弥漫——

"我发现了让空气香甜的另一方法：
绝望的另一种表达

"如今只剩下顶着星星的尖塔
大理石厅堂、庭院和海市蜃楼般的狂热在巴格达

"这些地方，以及你们熟悉的那些古迹
很快就没了，我正摧毁它们"

注释
① 这首诗发表在《卫报》上，讲述伊朗辉煌的历史古迹因为战争万劫不复。诗歌的最后几句说到死神正忙于占领巴格达。莫伸在接受BBC广播四台的采访时说，这首诗是他的政治宣言，意在"激烈地反战"。
② 尼尼微：意为"上帝面前最伟大的城市"。位于今天伊拉克北部城市摩苏尔附近，在底格里斯河东岸。该城市建立于公元前2500年左右。

附 录

附录是本书所选的英语战争诗歌的英语原文,方便英语爱好者参阅。

Robert Southey

After Blenheim

It was a summer evening,

Old Kaspar's work was done,

And he before his cottage door

Was sitting in the sun,

And by him sported on the green

His little grandchild Wilhelmine.

She saw her brother Peterkin

Roll something large and round,

Which he beside the rivulet

In playing there had found;

He came to ask what he had found,

That was so large, and smooth, and round.

Old Kaspar took it from the boy,

Who stood expectant by;

And then the old man shook his head,

And, with a natural sigh,

"'Tis some poor fellow's skull," said he,

"Who fell in the great victory.

"I find them in the garden,

For there's many here about;

And often when I go to plough,
The ploughshare turns them out!
For many thousand men," said he,
"Were slain in that great victory."
"Now tell us what 'twas all about,"
Young Peterkin, he cries;
And little Wilhelmine looks up
With wonder-waiting eyes;
"Now tell us all about the war,
And what they fought each other for."
"It was the English," Kaspar cried,
"Who put the French to rout;
But what they fought each other for
I could not well make out;
But everybody said,"quoth he,
"That 'twas a famous victory.
"My father lived at Blenheim then,
Yon little stream hard by;
They burnt his dwelling to the ground,
And he was forced to fly;
So with his wife and child he fled,
Nor had he where to rest his head.
"With fire and sword the country round
Was wasted far and wide,

And many a childing mother then,

And new-born baby died;

But things like that, you know, must be

At every famous victory.

"They say it was a shocking sight

After the field was won;

For many thousand bodies here

Lay rotting in the sun;

But things like that, you know, must be

After a famous victory.

"Great praise the Duke of Marlbro' won,

And our good Prince Eugene."

"Why, 'twas a very wicked thing!"

Said little Wilhelmine.

"Nay ... nay ... my little girl," quoth he,

"It was a famous victory."

"And everybody praised the Duke

Who this great fight did win."

"But what good came of it at last?"

Quoth little Peterkin.

"Why that I cannot tell," said he,

"But 'twas a famous victory."

Alfred Tennyson

The Charge of the Light Brigade

Half a league, half a league,

Half a league onward,

All in the valley of Death

Rode the six hundred.

"Forward, the Light Brigade!

Charge for the guns! " he said:

Into the valley of Death

Rode the six hundred.

"Forward, the Light Brigade! "

Was there a man dismay'd?

Not tho' the soldier knew

Some one had blunder'd:

Theirs not to make reply,

Theirs not to reason why,

Theirs but to do and die:

Into the valley of Death

Rode the six hundred.

Cannon to right of them,

Cannon to left of them,
Cannon in front of them
Volley'd and thunder'd;
Storm'd at with shot and shell,
Boldly they rode and well,
Into the jaws of Death,
Into the mouth of Hell
Rode the six hundred.

Flash'd all their sabres bare,
Flash'd as they turn'd in air
Sabring the gunners there,
Charging an army, while
All the world wonder'd:
Plunged in the battery-smoke
Right thro' the line they broke;
Cossack and Russian
Reel'd from the sabre-stroke
Shatter'd and sunder'd.
Then they rode back, but not
Not the six hundred.

Cannon to right of them,
Cannon to left of them,

Cannon behind them
Volley'd and thunder'd;
Storm'd at with shot and shell,
While horse and hero fell,
They that had fought so well
Came thro' the jaws of Death,
Back from the mouth of Hell,
All that was left of them,
Left of six hundred.

When can their glory fade?
O the wild charge they made!
All the world wonder'd.
Honor the charge they made!
Honor the Light Brigade,
Noble six hundred!

Walt Whitman

Beat! Beat! Drums!

Beat! beat! drums! —blow! bugles! blow!
Through the windows—through doors—burst like a ruthless force,
Into the solemn church, and scatter the congregation,
Into the school where the scholar is studying,
Leave not the bridegroom quiet—no happiness must he have now with his bride,
Nor the peaceful farmer any peace, ploughing his field or gathering his grain,
So fierce you whirr and pound you drums—so shrill you bugles blow.

Beat! beat! drums! —blow! bugles! blow!
Over the traffic of cities—over the rumble of wheels in the streets;
Are beds prepared for sleepers at night in the houses? no sleepers must sleep in those beds,
No bargainers' bargains by day—no brokers or speculators—would they continue?
Would the talkers be talking? would the singer attempt to sing?
Would the lawyer rise in the court to state his case before the judge?
Then rattle quicker, heavier drums—you bugles wilder blow.

Beat! beat! drums! —blow! bugles! blow!

Make no parley—stop for no expostulation,

Mind not the timid—mind not the weeper or prayer,

Mind not the old man beseeching the young man,

Let not the child's voice be heard, nor the mother's entreaties,

Make even the trestles to shake the dead where they lie awaiting the hearses,

So strong you thump O terrible drums—so loud you bugles blow.

Come Up from the Fields Father

Come up from the fields father, here's a letter from our Pete,

And come to the front door mother, here's a letter from thy dear son.

Lo, 'tis autumn,

Lo, where the trees, deeper green, yellower and redder,

Cool and sweeten Ohio's villages with leaves fluttering in the moderate wind,

Where apples ripe in the orchards hang and grapes on the trellis'd vines,

(Smell you the smell of the grapes on the vines?

Smell you the buckwheat where the bees were lately buzzing?)

Above all, lo, the sky so calm, so transparent after the rain, and with wondrous clouds,

Below too, all calm, all vital and beautiful, and the farm prospers well.

Down in the fields all prospers well,

But now from the fields come father, come at the daughter's call,

And come to the entry mother, to the front door come right away.

Fast as she can she hurries, something ominous, her steps trembling,

She does not tarry to smooth her hair nor adjust her cap.

Open the envelope quickly,

O this is not our son's writing, yet his name is sign'd,

O a strange hand writes for our dear son, O stricken mother's soul!

All swims before her eyes, flashes with black, she catches the main words only,

Sentences broken, *gunshot wound in the breast, cavalry skirmish, taken to hospital,*

At present low, but will soon be better.

Ah now the single figure to me,

Amid all teeming and wealthy Ohio with all its cities and farms,

Sickly white in the face and dull in the head, very faint,

By the jamb of a door leans.

Grieve not so, dear mother, (the just-grown daughter speaks through her sobs,
The little sisters huddle around speechless and dismay'd,)
See, dearest mother, the letter says Pete will soon be better.
Alas poor boy, he will never be better, (nor may-be needs to be better, that brave and simple soul,)
While they stand at home at the door he is dead already,
The only son is dead.

But the mother needs to be better,
She with thin form presently drest in black,
By day her meals untouch'd, then at night fitfully sleeping, often waking,
In the midnight waking, weeping, longing with one deep longing,
O that she might withdraw unnoticed, silent from life escape and withdraw,
To follow, to seek, to be with her dear dead son.

The Bravest Soldiers

Brave, brave were the soldiers (high named to-day) who lived through the fight;
But the bravest press'd to the front and fell, unnamed, unknown.

Emily Dickinson

It Feels a Shame to Be Alive

It feels a shame to be Alive—
When Men so brave—are dead—
One envies the Distinguished Dust—
Permitted—such a Head—

The Stone—that tells defending Whom
This Spartan put away
What little of Him we—possessed
In Pawn for Liberty—

The price is great Sublimely paid—
Do we deserve—a Thing—
That lives—like Dollars—must be piled
Before we may obtain?

Are we that wait sufficient worth—
That such Enormous Pearl
As life—dissolved be—for Us—
In Battle's—horrid Bowl?

It may be—a Renown to live—
I think the Man who die—
Those unsustained—Saviors—
Present Divinity—

Thomas Hardy

The Man He Killed

"Had he and I but met
    By some old ancient inn,
We should have set us down to wet
    Right many a nipperkin!

"But ranged as infantry,
    And staring face to face,
I shot at him as he at me,
    And killed him in his place.

"I shot him dead because —
    Because he was my foe,
Just so: my foe of course he was;
    That's clear enough; although

"He thought he 'd' list, perhaps,
    Off-hand like — just as I —
Was out of work — had sold his traps —
    No other reason why.

"Yes; quaint and curious war is!
 You shoot a fellow down
You'd treat if met where any bar is,
 Or help to half-a-crown."

Drummer Hodge

I

They throw in Drummer Hodge, to rest
 Uncoffined—just as found
His landmark is a kopje-crest
 That breaks the veldt around;
And foreign constellations west
 Each night above his mound.

II

Young Hodge the Drummer never knew—
 Fresh from his Wessex home—
The meaning of the broad Karoo,
 The Bush, the dusty loam,
And why uprose to nightly view
 Strange stars amid the gloam.

III

Yet portion of that unknown plain

Will Hodge forever be;
His homely Northern breast and brain
   Grow up a Southern tree,
And strange-eyed constellations reign
   His stars eternally.

In Time of 'The Breaking of Nations'

I

Only a man harrowing clods
   In a slow silent walk
With an old horse that stumbles and nods
   Half asleep as they stalk.

II

Only thin smoke without flame
   From the heaps of couch-grass;
Yet this will go onward the same
   Though Dynasties pass.

III

Yonder a maid and her wight
   Come whispering by:
War's annals will cloud into night
   Ere their story die.

Robert Louis Stevenson

Requiem

Under the wide and starry sky
Dig the grave and let me lie.
Glad did I live and gladly die,
And I laid me down with a will.

This be the verse you grave for me;
"Here he lies where he longed to be,
Home is the sailor, home from sea,
And the hunter home from the hill."

Alfred Edward Housman

Epitaph on an Army of Mercenaries

These, in the days when heaven was falling,
The hour when earth's foundations fled,
Followed their mercenary calling
And took their wages and are dead.

Their shoulders held the sky suspended;
They stood, and the earth's foundations stay;
What God abandoned, these defended,
And saved the sum of things for pay.

Here Dead We Lie

Here dead we lie
Because we did not choose
To live and shame the land
From which we sprung.
Life, to be sure,
Is nothing much to lose,
But young men think it is,
And we were young.

To an Athlete Dying Young

The time you won your town the race
We chaired you through the market-place;
Man and boy stood cheering by,
And home we brought you shoulder-high.

Today, the road all runners come,
Shoulder-high we bring you home,
And set you at your threshold down,
Townsman of a stiller town.

Smart lad, to slip betimes away
From fields where glory does not stay,
And early though the laurel grows
It withers quicker than the rose.

Eyes the shady night has shut
Cannot see the record cut,
And silence sounds no worse than cheers
After earth has stopped the ears.

Soldier from the Wars Returning

Soldier from the wars returning,
Spoiler of the taken town,
Here is ease that asks not earning;
Turn you in and sit you down.

Peace is come and wars are over,
Welcome you and welcome all,
While the charger crops the clover
And his bridle hangs in stall.

Now no more of winters biting,
Filth in trench from fall to spring,
Summers full of sweat and fighting
For the Kesar or the King.

Rest you, charger, rust you, bridle;
Kings and Kesars, keep your pay;
Soldier, sit you down and idle
At the inn of night for aye.

Katharine Tynan

Joining the Colours

There they go marching all in step so gay!
Smooth-cheeked and golden, food for shells and guns.
Blithely they go as to a wedding day,
The mothers' sons.

The drab street stares to see them row on row
On the high tram-tops, singing like the lark.
Too careless-gay for courage, singing they go
Into the dark.

With tin whistles, mouth-organs, any noise,
They pipe the way to glory and the grave;
Foolish and young, the gay and golden boys
Love cannot save.

High heart! High courage! The poor girls they kissed
Run with them : they shall kiss no more, alas!
Out of the mist they stepped-into the mist
Singing they pass.

William Butler Yeats

On Being Asked for a War Poem

I think it better that in times like these
A poet's mouth be silent, for in truth
We have no gift to set a statesman right;
He has had enough of meddling who can please
A young girl in the indolence of her youth,
Or an old man upon a winter's night.

Easter, 1916

...

Too long a sacrifice
Can make a stone of the heart.
O when may it suffice?

...

An Irish Airman Foresees His Death

I know that I shall meet my fate
Somewhere among the clouds above;

Those that I fight I do not hate,

Those that I guard I do not love;

My country is Kiltartan Cross,

My countrymen Kiltartan's poor,

No likely end could bring them loss

Or leave them happier than before.

Nor law, nor duty bade me fight,

Nor public men, nor cheering crowds,

A lonely impulse of delight

Drove to this tumult in the clouds;

I balanced all, brought all to mind,

The years to come seemed waste of breath,

A waste of breath the years behind

In balance with this life, this death.

Joseph Rudyard Kipling

Two Canadian Memorials

1914-18

I

We giving all gained all.

Neither lament us nor praise.

Only in all things recall,

It is Fear, not Death that slays.

II

From little towns in a far land we came,

To save our honour and a world aflame.

By little towns in a far land we sleep;

And trust that world we won for you to keep!

My Boy Jack

"Have you news of my boy Jack?"

Not this tide.

"When d'you think that he'll come back?"

Not with this wind blowing, and this tide.

"Has any one else had word of him?"

Not this tide.

For what is sunk will hardly swim,

Not with this wind blowing, and this tide.

"Oh, dear, what comfort can I find?"

None this tide,

Nor any tide,

Except he did not shame his kind —

Not even with that wind blowing, and that tide.

Then hold your head up all the more,

This tide,

And every tide;

Because he was the son you bore,

And gave to that wind blowing and that tide!

Common Form

1914-18

If any question why we died,

Tell them, because our fathers lied.

Unknown Female Corpse

1914-18

Headless, lacking foot and hand,

Horrible I come to land.

I beseech all women's sons

Know I was a mother once.

Salonikan Grave

1914-18

I have watched a thousand days

Push out and crawl into night

Slowly as tortoises.

Now I, too, follow these.

It is fever, and not the fight—

Time, not battle,—that slays.

An Only Son

1914-18

I have slain none except my Mother.

She (Blessing her slayer) died of grief for me.

Bombed in London

1914-18

On land and sea I strove with anxious care

To escape conscription. It was in the air!

Robert Laurence Binyon

For the Fallen

With proud thanksgiving, a mother for her children,
England mourns for her dead across the sea.
Flesh of her flesh they were, spirit of her spirit,
Fallen in the cause of the free.

Solemn the drums thrill: Death august and royal
Sings sorrow up into immortal spheres.
There is music in the midst of desolation
And a glory that shines upon our tears.

They went with songs to the battle, they were young,
Straight of limb, true of eye, steady and aglow.
They were staunch to the end against odds uncounted,
They fell with their faces to the foe.

They shall grow not old, as we that are left grow old:
Age shall not weary them, nor the years condemn.
At the going down of the sun and in the morning
We will remember them.

They mingle not with their laughing comrades again;
They sit no more at familiar tables of home;
They have no lot in our labour of the day-time;
They sleep beyond England's foam.

But where our desires are and our hopes profound,
Felt as a well-spring that is hidden from sight,
To the innermost heart of their own land they are known
As the stars are known to the Night;

As the stars that shall be bright when we are dust,
Moving in marches upon the heavenly plain,
As the stars that are starry in the time of our darkness,
To the end, to the end, they remain.

Charlotte Mary Mew

The Cenotaph

Not yet will those measureless fields be green again
Where only yesterday the wild sweet blood of wonderful youth was shed;
There is a grave whose earth must hold too long, too deep a stain,
Though for ever over it we may speak as proudly as we may tread.
But here, where the watchers by lonely hearths from the thrust of an inward sword have more slowly bled,
We shall build the Cenotaph: Victory, winged, with Peace, winged too, at the column's head.
And over the stairway, at the foot—oh! here, leave desolate, passionate hands to spread
Violets, roses, and laurel with the small sweet twinkling country things
Speaking so wistfully of other Springs
From the little gardens of little places where son or sweetheart was born and bred.
In splendid sleep, with a thousand brothers
To lovers—to mothers
Here, too, lies he:
Under the purple, the green, the red,
It is all young life: it must break some women's hearts to see

Such a brave, gay coverlet to such a bed!

Only, when all is done and said,

God is not mocked and neither are the dead.

For this will stand in our Market-place—

Who'll sell, who'll buy

(Will you or I

Lie each to each with the better grace)?

While looking into every busy whore's and huckster's face

As they drive their bargains, is the Face

Of God: and some young, piteous, murdered face.

John McCrae

In Flanders Fields

In Flanders fields the poppies blow
Between the crosses, row on row
That mark our place; and in the sky
The larks, still bravely singing, fly
Scarce heard amid the guns below.
We are the Dead. Short days ago
We lived, felt dawn, saw sunset glow,
Loved and were loved, and now we lie
In Flanders fields.
Take up our quarrel with the foe:
To you from failing hands we throw
The torch; be yours to hold it high.
If ye break faith with us who die
We shall not sleep, though poppies grow
In Flanders fields.

Walter John de la Mare

Napoleon

'What is the world, O soldiers?

It is I:

I, this incessant snow,

This northern sky;

Soldiers, this solitude

Through which we go

Is I.'

Robert Service

The Twins

There were two brothers, John and James,
And when the town went up in flames,
To save the house of James dashed John,
Then turned, and lo! his own was gone.

And when the great World War began,
To volunteer John promptly ran;
And while he learned live bombs to lob,
James stayed at home and—sneaked his job.

John came home with a missing limb;
That didn't seem to worry him;
But oh, it set his brain awhirl
To find that James had—sneaked his girl!

Time passed. John tried his grief to drown;
To-day James owns one-half the town;
His army contracts riches yield;
And John? Well, search the Potter's Field.

G · K · Chesterton

Elegy in a Country Courtyard

The men that worked for England
They have their graves at home:
And birds and bees of England
About the cross can roam.

But they that fought for England,
Following a falling star,
Alas, alas for England
They have their graves afar.

And they that rule in England,
In stately conclave met,
Alas, alas for England
They have no graves as yet.

Carl Sandburg

A. E. F.

There will be a rusty gun on the wall, sweetheart,

The rifle grooves curling with flakes of rust.

A spider will make a silver string nest in the

darkest, warmest corner of it.

The trigger and the range-finder, they too will be rusty.

And no hands will polish the gun, and it will hang on the wall.

Forefingers and thumbs will point casually toward it.

It will be spoken among half-forgotten, whished-to-be-forgotten things.

They will tell the spider: Go on, you're doing good work.

A.E.F.: *American expeditionary forces.*

Grass

Pile the bodies high at Austerlitz and Waterloo.

Shovel them under and let me work—

                I am the grass; I cover all.

And pile them high at Gettysburg

And pile them high at Ypres and Verdun.

Shovel them under and let me work.

Two years, ten years, and passengers ask the conductor:

    What place is this?

    Where are we now?

    I am the grass.

    Let me work.

And They Obey

Smash down the cities.

Knock the walls to pieces.

Break the factories and cathedrals, warehouses and homes

Into loose piles of stone and lumber and black burnt wood:

You are the soldiers and we command you.

Build up the cities.

Set up the walls again.

Put together once more the factories and cathedrals, warehouses and homes

Into buildings for life and labor:

You are workmen and citizens all: We command you.

Philip Edwards Thomas

The Trumpet

Rise up, rise up,

And, as the trumpet blowing

Chases the dreams of men,

As the dawn glowing

The stars that left unlit

The land and water,

Rise up and scatter

The dew that covers

The print of last night's lovers—

Scatter it, scatter it!

While you are listening

To the clear horn,

Forget, men, everything

On this earth newborn,

Except that it is lovelier

Than any mysteries.

Open your eyes to the air

That has washed the eyes of the stars

Through all the dewy night:

Up with the light,

To the old wars;

Arise, arise!

This Is No Case of Petty Right or Wrong

This is no case of petty right or wrong

That politicians or philosophers

Can judge. I hate not Germans, nor grow hot

With love of Englishmen, to please newspapers.

Beside my hate for one fat patriot

My hatred of the Kaiser is love true —

A kind of god he is, banging a gong.

But I have not to choose between the two,

Or between justice and injustice. Dinned

With war and argument I read no more

Than in the storm smoking along the wind

Athwart the wood. Two witches' cauldrons roar.

From one the weather shall rise clear and gay;

Out of the other an England beautiful

And like her mother that died yesterday.

Little I know or care if, being dull,

I shall miss something that historians

Can rake out of the ashes when perchance

The phoenix broods serene above their ken.
But with the best and meanest Englishmen
I am one in crying, God save England, lest
We lose what never slaves and cattle blessed.
The ages made her that made us from dust:
She is all we know and live by, and we trust
She is good and must endure, loving her so:
And as we love ourselves we hate our foe.

Wilfrid Wilson Gibson

Breakfast

We ate our breakfast lying on our backs,

Because the shells were screeching overhead.

I bet a rasher to a loaf of bread

That Hull United would beat Halifax

When Jimmy Stainthorpe played full-back instead

of Billy Bradford. Ginger raised his head

And cursed, and took the bet; and dropt back dead.

We ate our breakfast lying on our backs,

Because the shells were screeching overhead.

The Messages

"I cannot quite remember... There were five

Dropt dead beside me in the trench—and three

Whispered their dying messages to me..."

Back from the trenches, more dead than alive,

Stone-deaf and dazed, and with a broken knee,

He hobbled slowly, muttering vacantly:

"I cannot quite remember.... There were five
Dropt dead beside me in the trench, and three
Whispered their dying messages to me...

"Their friends are waiting, wondering how they thrive—
Waiting a word in silence patiently...
But what they said, or who their friends may be

"I cannot quite remember... There where five
Dropt dead beside me in the trench—and three
Whispered their dying messages to me..."

Wallace Stevens

Phases

I.

There's a little square in Paris,

Waiting until we pass.

They sit idly there,

They sip the glass.

There's a cab-horse at the corner,

There's rain. The season grieves.

It was silver once,

And green with leaves.

There's a parrot in a window,

Will see us on parade,

Hear the loud drums roll—

And serenade.

II.

This was the salty taste of glory,

That it was not

Like Agamemnon's story.

Only, an eyeball in the mud,

And Hopkins,

Flat and pale and gory!

III.

But the bugles, in the night,

Were wings that bore

To where our comfort was;

Arabesques of candle beams,

Winding

Through our heavy dreams;

Winds that blew

Where the bending iris grew;

Birds of intermitted bliss,

Singing in the night's abyss;

Vines with yellow fruit,

That fell

Along the walls

That bordered Hell.

IV.

Death's nobility again

Beautified the simplest men.

Fallen Winkle felt the pride

Of Agamemnon

When he died.

What could London's

Work and waste

Give him—

To that salty, sacrificial taste?

What could London's

Sorrow bring—

To that short, triumphant sting?

Sara Teasdale

Spring in War-Time

I feel the spring far off, far off,
    The faint, far scent of bud and leaf—
Oh, how can spring take heart to come
    To a world in grief,
        Deep grief?

The sun turns north, the days grow long,
    Later the evening star grows bright—
How can the daylight linger on
    For men to fight,
        Still fight?

The grass is waking in the ground,
    Soon it will rise and blow in waves—
How can it have the heart to sway
    Over the graves,
        New graves?

Under the boughs where lovers walked
    The apple-blooms will shed their breath—

But what of all the lovers now
   Parted by Death,
Grey Death?

Ezra Pound

Hugh Selwyn Mauberley

III

All men, in law, are equals.

Free of Peisistratus,

We choose a knave or an eunuch

To rule over us.

A bright Apollo,

tin andra, tin eroa, tina theon,

What god, man, or hero

Shall I place a tin wreath upon?

IV

These fought, in any case,

and some believing, pro domo, in any case ...

Some quick to arm,

some for adventure,

some from fear of weakness,

some from fear of censure,

some for love of slaughter, in imagination,

learning later ...

some in fear, learning love of slaughter;

Died some pro patria, non dulce non et decor" ...

walked eye-deep in hell

believing in old men's lies, then unbelieving

came home, home to a lie,

home to many deceits,

home to old lies and new infamy;

usury age-old and age-thick

and liars in public places.

Daring as never before, wastage as never before.

Young blood and high blood,

Fair cheeks, and fine bodies;

fortitude as never before

frankness as never before,

disillusions as never told in the old days,

hysterias, trench confessions,

laughter out of dead bellies.

V

There died a myriad,

And of the best, among them,

For an old bitch gone in the teeth,

For a botched civilization.

Charm, smiling at the good mouth,

Quick eyes gone under earth's lid,

For two gross of broken statues,

For a few thousand battered books.

...

Siegfried Sassoon

Does It Matter?

Does it matter? — losing your leg? ...
For people will always be kind,
And you need not show that you mind
When the others come in after hunting
To gobble their muffins and eggs.

Does it matter? — losing your sight? ...
There's such splendid work for the blind;
And people will always be kind,
As you sit on the terrace remembering
And turning your face to the light.

Do they matter? — those dreams from the pit? ...
You can drink and forget and be glad,
And people won't say that you're mad;
For they'll know that you've fought for your country,
And no one will worry a bit.

Base Details

If I were fierce, and bald, and short of breath,

I'd live with scarlet Majors at the Base,

And speed glum heroes up the line to death.

You'd see me with my puffy petulant face,

Guzzling and gulping in the best hotel,

Reading the Roll of Honour. "Poor young chap,"

I'd say—"I used to know his father well.

Yes, we've lost heavily in this last scrap."

And when the war is done and youth stone dead,

I'd toddle safely home and die—in bed

In Me, Past, Present, Future Meet

In me, past, present, future meet

To hold long chiding conference.

My lusts usurp the present tense

And strangle Reason in his seat.

My loves leap through the future's fence

To dance with dream-enfranchised feet.

In me the cave-man clasps the seer,

And garlanded Apollo goes

Chanting to Abraham's deaf ear.

In me the tiger sniffs the rose.

Look in my heart, kind friends, and tremble,

Since there your elements assemble.

To Any Dead Officer

Well, how are things in Heaven? I wish you'd say,
    Because I'd like to know that you're all right.
Tell me, have you found everlasting day,
    Or been sucked in by everlasting night?
For when I shut my eyes your face shows plain;
    I hear you make some cheery old remark—
I can rebuild you in my brain,
    Though you've gone out patrolling in the dark.

You hated tours of trenches; you were proud
    Of nothing more than having good years to spend;
Longed to get home and join the careless crowd
    Of chaps who work in peace with Time for friend.
That's all washed out now. You're beyond the wire:
    No earthly chance can send you crawling back;
You've finished with machine-gun fire—
    Knocked over in a hopeless dud-attack.

Somehow I always thought you'd get done in,

   Because you were so desperate keen to live:

You were all out to try and save your skin,

   Well knowing how much the world had got to give.

You joked at shells and talked the usual "shop,"

   Stuck to your dirty job and did it fine:

With "Jesus Christ! when will it stop?

   Three years ... It's hell unless we break their line."

So when they told me you'd been left for dead

   I wouldn't believe them, feeling it must be true.

Next week the bloody Roll of Honour said

   "Wounded and missing"— That's the thing to do

When lads are left in shell-holes dying slow,

   With nothing but blank sky and wounds that ache,

Moaning for water till they know

   It's night, and then it's not worth while to wake!

Good-bye, old lad! Remember me to God,

   And tell Him that our politicians swear

They won't give in till Prussian Rule's been trod

   Under the Heel of England ... Are you there? ...

Yes ... and the war won't end for at least two years;

But we've got stacks of men ... I'm blind with tears,

Staring into the dark. Cheero!
I wish they'd killed you in a decent show.

The Death Bed

He drowsed and was aware of silence heaped
Round him, unshaken as the steadfast walls;
Aqueous like floating rays of amber light,
Soaring and quivering in the wings of sleep.
Silence and safety; and his mortal shore
Lipped by the inward, moonless waves of death.

Someone was holding water to his mouth.
He swallowed, unresisting; moaned and dropped
Through crimson gloom to darkness; and forgot
The opiate throb and ache that was his wound.
Water—calm, sliding green above the weir;
Water—a sky-lit alley for his boat,
Bird-voiced, and bordered with reflected flowers
And shaken hues of summer: drifting down,
He dipped contented oars, and sighed, and slept.

Night, with a gust of wind, was in the ward,
Blowing the curtain to a gummering curve.

Night. He was blind; he could not see the stars
Glinting among the wraiths of wandering cloud;
Queer blots of colour, purple, scarlet, green,
Flickered and faded in his drowning eyes.

Rain—he could hear it rustling through the dark;
Fragrance and passionless music woven as one;
Warm rain on drooping roses; pattering showers
That soak the woods; not the harsh rain that sweeps
Behind the thunder, but a trickling peace,
Gently and slowly washing life away.

He stirred, shifting his body; then the pain
Leaped like a prowling beast, and gripped and tore
His groping dreams with grinding claws and fangs.
But someone was beside him; soon he lay
Shuddering because that evil thing had passed.
And death, who'd stepped toward him, paused and stared.

Light many lamps and gather round his bed.
Lend him your eyes, warm blood, and will to live.
Speak to him; rouse him; you may save him yet.
He's young; he hated war; how should he die
When cruel old campaigners win safe through?

But death replied: "I choose him." So he went,
And there was silence in the summer night;
Silence and safety; and the veils of sleep.
Then, far away, the thudding of the guns.

Repression of War Experience

Now light the candles; one; two; there's a moth;
What silly beggars they are to blunder in
And scorch their wings with glory, liquid flame—
No, no, not that,—it's bad to think of war,
When thoughts you've gagged all day come back to scare you;
And it's been proved that soldiers don't go mad
Unless they lose control of ugly thoughts
That drive them out to jabber among the trees.

Now light your pipe; look, what a steady hand.
Draw a deep breath; stop thinking; count fifteen,
And you're as right as rain ...
 Why won't it rain? ...
I wish there'd be a thunder-storm to-night,
With bucketsful of water to sluice the dark,
And make the roses hang their dripping heads.

Books; what a jolly company they are,
Standing so quiet and patient on their shelves,
Dressed in dim brown, and black, and white, and green,
And every kind of colour. Which will you read?
Come on; O do read something; they're so wise.
I tell you all the wisdom of the world
Is waiting for you on those shelves; and yet
You sit and gnaw your nails, and let your pipe out,
And listen to the silence: on the ceiling
There's one big, dizzy moth that bumps and flutters;
And in the breathless air outside the house
The garden waits for something that delays.
There must be crowds of ghosts among the trees,—
Not people killed in battle,—they're in France,—
But horrible shapes in shrouds—old men who died
Slow, natural deaths,—old men with ugly souls,
Who wore their bodies out with nasty sins.

You're quiet and peaceful, summering safe at home;
You'd never think there was a bloody war on! ...
O yes, you would ... why, you can hear the guns.
Hark! Thud, thud, thud,—quite soft ... they never cease—
Those whispering guns—O Christ, I want to go out
And screech at them to stop—I'm going crazy;
I'm going stark, staring mad because of the guns.

Absolution

The anguish of the earth absolves our eyes
Till beauty shines in all that we can see.
War is our scourge; yet war has made us wise,
And, fighting for our freedom, we are free.

Horror of wounds and anger at the foe,
And loss of things desired; all these must pass.
We are the happy legion, for we know
Time's but a golden wind that shakes the grass.

There was an hour when we were loth to part
From life we longed to share no less than others.
Now, having claimed this heritage of heart,
What need we more, my comrades and my brothers?

Dreamers

Soldiers are citizens of death's grey land,
Drawing no dividend from time's to-morrows.
In the great hour of destiny they stand,
Each with his feuds, and jealousies, and sorrows.
Soldiers are sworn to action; they must win
Some flaming, fatal climax with their lives.

Soldiers are dreamers; when the guns begin
They think of firelit homes, clean beds and wives.

I see them in foul dug-outs, gnawed by rats,
And in the ruined trenches, lashed with rain,
Dreaming of things they did with balls and bats,
And mocked by hopeless longing to regain
Bank-holidays, and picture shows, and spats,
And going to the office in the train.

'They'

The Bishop tells us: 'When the boys come back
'They will not be the same; for they'll have fought
'In a just cause: they lead the last attack
'On Anti-Christ; their comrades' blood has bought
'New right to breed an honourable race,
'They have challenged Death and dared him face to face.'

'We're none of us the same! ' the boys reply.
'For George lost both his legs; and Bill's stone blind;
'Poor Jim's shot through the lungs and like to die;
'And Bert's gone syphilitic: you'll not find
'A chap who's served that hasn't found some change.

' And the Bishop said: 'The ways of God are strange

Suicide in the Trenches

I knew a simple soldier boy

Who grinned at life in empty joy,

Slept soundly through the lonesome dark,

And whistled early with the lark.

In winter trenches, cowed and glum,

With crumps and lice and lack of rum,

He put a bullet through his brain.

No one spoke of him again.

You smug-faced crowds with kindling eye

Who cheer when soldier lads march by,

Sneak home and pray you'll never know

The hell where youth and laughter go.

Rupert Brooke

The Soldier

    If I should die, think only of me:
      That there's some corner of a foreign field
That is for ever England. There shall be
    In that rich earth a richer dust concealed;
A dust whom England bore, shaped, made aware,
      Gave, once, her flowers to love, her ways to roam;
A body of England's, breathing English air,
    Washed by the rivers, blest by suns of home.

And think, this heart, all evil shed away,
    A pulse in the eternal mind, no less
        Gives somewhere back the thoughts by England given;
Her sights and sounds; dreams happy as her day;
  And laughter, learnt of friends; and gentleness,
      In hearts at peace, under an English heaven.

The Dead

These hearts were woven of human joys and cares,
    Washed marvellously with sorrow, swift to mirth.
The years had given them kindness. Dawn was theirs,

  And sunset, and the colours of the earth.
These had seen movement, and heard music; known
  Slumber and waking; loved; gone proudly friended;
Felt the quick stir of wonder; sat alone;
  Touched flowers and furs and cheeks. All this is ended.

There are waters blown by changing winds to laughter
And lit by the rich skies, all day. And after,
  Frost, with a gesture, stays the waves that dance
And wandering loveliness. He leaves a white
  Unbroken glory, a gathered radiance,
A width, a shining peace, under the night.

Elizabeth Daryush

For a Survivor of the Mesopotamian Campaign

War's wasted era is a desert shore,
As know those who have passed there, a place

Where, within sound of swoll'n destruction's roar,
Wheel the wild vultures, lust and terror base;
Where, making ready for them, stalk the grim
Barbarian forms, hunger, disease and pain,
Who, slashing all life's beauty limb from limb,
Crush it as folly on the stony plain.

A desert: – those too who, as thou, have been
Followers of war's angel, Sacrifice,
(Stern striders to beyond brute torment's scene,
Soarers above the swerves of fear and vice)
Know that the lightning of his ghostly gaze
Has wrecked for them for ever earth's small ways.

Alan Seeger

I Have a Rendezvous with Death

I have a rendezvous with Death
At some disputed barricade,
When Spring comes back with rustling shade
And apple-blossoms fill the air—
I have a rendezvous with Death
When Spring brings back blue days and fair.

It may be he shall take my hand
And lead me into his dark land
And close my eyes and quench my breath—
It may be I shall pass him still.
I have a rendezvous with Death
On some scarred slope of battered hill,
When Spring comes round again this year
And the first meadow-flowers appear.

God knows 'twere better to be deep
Pillowed in silk and scented down,
Where Love throbs out in blissful sleep,
Pulse nigh to pulse, and breath to breath,

Where hushed awakenings are dear ...
But I've a rendezvous with Death
At midnight in some flaming town,
When Spring trips north again this year,
And I to my pledged word am true,
I shall not fail that rendezvous.

Ivor Gurney

To His Love

He's gone, and all our plans
    Are useless indeed.
We'll walk no more on Cotswold
    Where the sheep feed
    Quietly and take no heed.

His body that was so quick
    Is not as you
Knew it, on Severn river
    Under the blue
    Driving our small boat through.

You would not know him now ...
    But still he died
Nobly, so cover him over
    With violets of pride
    Purple from Severn side.

Cover him, cover him soon!
    And with thick-set

Masses of memoried flowers—

Hide that red wet

Thing I must somehow forget.

Isaac Rosenberg

The Troop Ship

Grotesque and queerly huddled

Contortionists to twist

The sleepy soul to a sleep,

We lie all sorts of ways

And cannot sleep.

The wet wind is so cold,

And the lurching men so careless,

That, should you drop to a doze,

Wind's fumble or men's feet

Is on your face.

Richard Aldington

War Yawp

America!

England's cheeky kid brother,

Who bloodily assaulted your august elder

At Bunker Hill and similar places

(Not mentioned in our history books),

What can I tell you of war or of peace?

Say, have you forgotten 1861?

Bull Run, Gettysburg, Fredericksburg?

Your million dead?

Tell me,

Was that the greatest time of your lives

Or the most disastrous?

Who knows? Not you; not I.

Who can tell the end of this war?

And say, brother Jonathan,

D'you know what it's all about?

Let me whisper you a secret—we don't!

We were all too fat with peace,

Or perhaps we didn't quite know how good peace was,

And so here we are,

And we're going to win....

It's fine to be a soldier,

To get accepted by the recruiting sergeant,

Be trained, fitted with a uniform and a gun,

Say good-bye to your girl,

And go off to the front

Whistling, "It's a long way to Tipperary."

It's good to march forty miles a day,

Carrying ninety-one pounds on your back,

To eat good coarse food, get blistered, tired out, wounded,

Thirst, starve, fight like a devil

(i. e., like you an' me, Jonathan),

With the Maxims zip-zipping

And the shrapnel squealing,

And the howitzers rumbling like the traffic in Piccadilly.

Civilization?—

Jonathan, if you could hear them

Whistling the *Marseillaise* or *Marching Through Georgia*,

You'd want to go too.

Twenty thousand a day, Jonathan!

Perhaps you're more civilized just now than we are,

Perhaps we've only forgotten civilization for a moment,

Perhaps we're really fighting for peace.

And after all it will be more fun afterwards—

More fun for the poets and the painters—

When the cheering's all over

And the dead men buried

And the rest gone back to their jobs.

It'll be more fun for them to make their patterns,

Their word-patterns and color-patterns.

And after all, there is always war and always peace,

Always the war of the crowds,

Always the great peace of the arts.

Even now,

With the war beating in great waves overhead,

Beating and roaring like great winds and mighty waters,

The sea-gods still pattern the red seaweed fronds,

Still chip the amber into neck-chains

For Leucothea and Thetis.

Even now,

When the *Marseillaise* screams like a hurt woman,

And Paris—grisette among cities—trembles with fear,

The poets still make their music

Which nobody listens to,

Which hardly anyone ever listened to.

The great crowds go by,
Fighting over each other's bodies in peace-time,
Fighting over each other's bodies in war-time.
Something of the strife comes to them
In their little, high rock-citadel of art,
Where they hammer their dreams in gold and copper,
Where they cut them in pine-wood, in Parian stone, in wax,
Where they sing them in sweet bizarre words
To the sound of antiquated shrill instruments;
And they are happy.

The little rock-citadel of the artists
Is always besieged;
There, though they have beauty and silence,
They have always tears and hunger and despair.
But that little citadel has held out
Against all the wars of the world—
Like England, brother Jonathan.
It will not fall during the great war.

There is always war and always peace;
Always the war of the crowds,
Always the great peace of the arts.

Trench Idyll

We sat together in the trench,

He on a lump of frozen earth

Blown in the night before,

I on an unexploded shell;

And smoked and talked, like exiles,

Of how pleasant London was,

Its women, restaurants, night clubs, theatres,

How at that very hour

The taxi-cabs were taking folk to dine...

Then we sat silent for a while

As a machine-gun swept the parapet.

He said:

'I've been here on and off two years

And seen only one man killed'.

'That's odd.'

'The bullet hit him in the throat;

He fell in a heap on the fire-step,

And called out "My God! dead! "

'Good Lord, how terrible! '

'Well, as to that, the nastiest job I've had

Was last year on this very front

Taking the discs at night from men

Who'd hung for six months on the wire

Just over there.

The worst of all was

They fell to pieces at a touch.

Thank God we couldn't see their faces;

They had gas helmets on...'

I shivered;

'It's rather cold here, sir, suppose we move?'

Wilfred Owen

Strange Meeting

It seemed that out of battle I escaped
Down some profound dull tunnel, long since scooped
Through granites which titanic wars had groined.

Yet also there encumbered sleepers groaned,
Too fast in thought or death to be bestirred.
Then, as I probed them, one sprang up, and stared
With piteous recognition in fixed eyes,
Lifting distressful hands, as if to bless.
And by his smile, I knew that sullen hall,—
By his dead smile I knew we stood in Hell.

With a thousand fears that vision's face was grained;
Yet no blood reached there from the upper ground,
And no guns thumped, or down the flues made moan.
"Strange friend," I said, "here is no cause to mourn."
"None," said that other, "save the undone years,
The hopelessness. Whatever hope is yours,
Was my life also; I went hunting wild
After the wildest beauty in the world,

Which lies not calm in eyes, or braided hair,
But mocks the steady running of the hour,
And if it grieves, grieves richlier than here.
For by my glee might many men have laughed,
And of my weeping something had been left,
Which must die now. I mean the truth untold,
The pity of war, the pity war distilled.
Now men will go content with what we spoiled.
Or, discontent, boil bloody, and be spilled.
They will be swift with swiftness of the tigress.
None will break ranks, though nations trek from progress.
Courage was mine, and I had mystery;
Wisdom was mine, and I had mastery:
To miss the march of this retreating world
Into vain citadels that are not walled.
Then, when much blood had clogged their chariot-wheels,
I would go up and wash them from sweet wells,
Even with truths that lie too deep for taint.
I would have poured my spirit without stint
But not through wounds; not on the cess of war.
Foreheads of men have bled where no wounds were.

"I am the enemy you killed, my friend.
I knew you in this dark: for so you frowned

Yesterday through me as you jabbed and killed.

I parried; but my hands were loath and cold.

Let us sleep now..."

Futility

Move him into the sun—
Gently its touch awoke him once,
At home, whispering of fields half-sown.
Always it awoke him, even in France,
Until this morning and this snow.
If anything might rouse him now
The kind old sun will know.

Think how it wakes the seeds—
Woke once the clays of a cold star.
Are limbs, so dear-achieved, are sides
Full-nerved, still warm, too hard to stir?
Was it for this the clay grew tall?
—O, what made fatuous sunbeams toil
To break earth's sleep at all?

S. I. W.

> I will to the King,
>
> And offer him consolation in his trouble,
>
> For that man there has set his teeth to die,
>
> And being one that hates obedience,
>
> Discipline, and orderliness of life,
>
> I cannot mourn him.
>
> ——W.B. YEATS

I. THE PROLOGUE

Patting good-bye, doubtless they told the lad

He'd always show the Hun a brave man's face;

Father would sooner him dead than in disgrace,—

Was proud to see him going, aye, and glad.

Perhaps his mother whimpered how she'd fret

Until he got a nice, safe wound to nurse.

Sisters would wish girls too could shoot, charge, curse, ...

Brothers—would send his favourite cigarette.

Each week, month after month, they wrote the same,

Thinking him sheltered in some Y.M. Hut,

Because he said so, writing on his butt

Where once an hour a bullet missed its aim

And misses teased the hunger of his brain.

His eyes grew old with wincing, and his hand

Reckless with ague. Courage leaked, as sand

From the best sandbags after years of rain.

But never leave, wound, fever, trench-foot, shock,

Untrapped the wretch. And death seemed still withheld

For torture of lying machinally shelled,

At the pleasure of this world's Powers who'd run amok.

He'd seen men shoot their hands, on night patrol.

Their people never knew. Yet they were vile.

'Death sooner than dishonour, that's the style!'

So Father said.

II. THE ACTION

One dawn, our wire patrol

Carried him. This time, Death had not missed.

We could do nothing but wipe his bleeding cough.

Could it be accident? —— Rifles go off...

Not sniped? No. (Later they found the English ball.)

III. THE POEM

It was the reasoned crisis of his soul

Against more days of inescapable thrall,

Against infrangibly wired and blind trench wall

Curtained with fire, roofed in with creeping fire,

Slow grazing fire, that would not burn him whole

But kept him for death's promises and scoff,

And life's half-promising, and both their riling.

IV. THE EPILOGUE

With him they buried the muzzle his teeth had kissed,

And truthfully wrote the Mother, 'Tim died smiling'.

Dulce et Decorum Est

Bent double, like old beggars under sacks,

Knock-kneed, coughing like hags, we cursed through sludge,

Till on the haunting flares we turned our backs,

And towards our distant rest began to trudge.

Men marched asleep. Many had lost their boots,

But limped on, blood-shod. All went lame; all blind;

Drunk with fatigue; deaf even to the hoots

Of gas-shells dropping softly behind.

Gas! GAS! Quick, boys! —An ecstasy of fumbling

Fitting the clumsy helmets just in time,

But someone still was yelling out and stumbling

And flound'ring like a man in fire or lime.—

Dim through the misty panes and thick green light,

As under a green sea, I saw him drowning.

In all my dreams before my helpless sight,
He plunges at me, guttering, choking, drowning.

If in some smothering dreams, you too could pace
Behind the wagon that we flung him in,
And watch the white eyes writhing in his face,
His hanging face, like a devil's sick of sin;
If you could hear, at every jolt, the blood
Come gargling from the froth-corrupted lungs,
Obscene as cancer, bitter as the cud
Of vile, incurable sores on innocent tongues,—
My friend, you would not tell with such high zest
To children ardent for some desperate glory,
The old Lie: *Dulce et decorum est*
Pro patria mori.

Anthem for Doomed Youth

What passing-bells for these who die as cattle?
Only the monstrous anger of the guns.
Only the stuttering rifles' rapid rattle.
Can patter out their hasty orisons.

No mockeries for them; no prayers nor bells,
Nor any voice of mourning save the choirs,
The shrill, demented choirs of wailing shells;
And bugles calling for them from sad shires.

What candles may be held to speed them all?
Not in the hands of boys, but in their eyes
Shall shine the holy glimmers of goodbyes.

The pallor of girls' brows shall be their pall;
Their flowers the tenderness of patient minds,
And each slow dusk a drawing-down of blinds.

Dame Margaret Isabel Postgate Cole DBE

The Falling Leaves

Today, as I rode by,

I saw the brown leaves dropping from their tree

In a still afternoon,

When no wind whirled them whistling to the sky,

But thickly, silently,

They fell, like snowflakes wiping out the noon;

And wandered slowly thence

For thinking of a gallant multitude

Which now all withering lay,

Slain by no wind of age or pestilence,

But in their beauty strewed

Like snowflakes falling on the Flemish clay.

The Veteran

We came upon him sitting in the sun

Blinded by war, and left. And past the fence

There came young soldiers from the Hand and Flower,

Asking advice of his experience.

And he said this, and that, and told them tales,

And all the nightmares of each empty head

Blew into air; then, hearing us beside,

"Poor chaps, how'd they know what it's like?" he said.

And we stood there, and watched him as he sat,

Turning his sockets where they went away,

Until it came to one of us to ask "And you're-how old?"

"Nineteen, the third of May."

Dorothy Parker

The Veteran

When I was young and bold and strong,

Oh, right was right, and wrong was wrong!

My plume on high, my flag unfurled,

I rode away to right the world.

"Come out, your dogs, and fight!" said I,

And wept there was but once to die.

But I am old; and good and bad

Are woven in a crazy plaid

I sit and say, "The world is so;

And he is wise who lets it go.

A battle lost, a battle won—

The difference is small, my son."

Inertia rides and riddles me;

The which is called Philosophy.

May Wedderburn Cannan

August 1914

The sun rose over the sweep of the hill
　All bare for the gathered hay,
And a blackbird sang by the window-sill,
　And a girl knelt down to pray:
　　'Whom Thou hast kept through the night, O Lord,
　　Keep Thou safe through the day.'

The sun rose over the shell-swept height,
　The guns are over the way,
And a soldier turned from the toil of the night
　To the toil of another day,
　　And a bullet sang by the parapet
　　To drive in the new-turned clay.

The sun sank slow by the sweep of the hill,
　They had carried all the hay,
And a blackbird sang by the window-sill,
　And a girl knelt down to pray:
　　'Keep Thou safe through the night, O Lord,
　　Whom Thou hast kept through the day.'

The sun sank slow by the shell-swept height,
  The guns had prepared a way,
And a soldier turned to sleep that night
  Who would not wake for the day,
    And a blackbird flew from the window-sill,
    When a girl knelt down to pray.

After the War

After the war perhaps I'll sit again
Out on the terrace where I sat with you,
And see the changeless sky and hills beat blue
And live an afternoon of summer through.

I shall remember then, and sad at heart
For the lost day of happiness we knew,
Wish only that some other man were you
And spoke my name as once you used to do.

Vera Brittain

Perhaps (To R.A.L.)

Perhaps some day the sun will shine again,

And I shall see that still the skies are blue,

And feel once more I do not live in vain,

Although bereft of You.

Perhaps the golden meadows at my feet

Will make the sunny hours of spring seem gay,

And I shall find the white May-blossoms sweet,

Though You have passed away.

Perhaps the summer woods will shimmer bright,

And crimson roses once again be fair,

And autumn harvest fields a rich delight,

Although You are not there.

Perhaps some day I shall not shrink in pain

To see the passing of the dying year,

And listen to Christmas songs again,

Although You cannot hear.

But though kind Time may many joys renew,
There is one greatest joy I shall not know
Again, because my heart for loss of You
Was broken, long ago.

Roundel

(*Died of Wounds*)

Because you died, I shall not rest again,
    But wander ever through the lone world wide,
Seeking the shadow of a dream grown vain
        Because you died.

I shall spend brief and idle hours beside
    The many lesser loves that still remain,
But find in none my triumph and my pride;

And Disillusion's slow corroding stain
    Will creep upon each quest but newly tried,
For every striving now shall nothing gain
        Because you died.

August, 1914

God said, "Men have forgotten Me:
The souls that sleep shall wake again,
   And blinded eyes must learn to see."

So since redemption comes through pain
He smote the earth with chastening rod,
   And brought destruction's lurid reign;

But where His desolation trod
The people in their agony
   Despairing cried, "There is no God."

Charles Hamilton Sorley

Such, Such Is Death

Such, such is Death: no triumph: no defeat:
Only an empty pail, a slate rubbed clean,
A merciful putting away of what has been.

And this we know: Death is not Life, effete,
Life crushed, the broken pail. We who have seen
So marvellous things know well the end not yet.

Victor and vanquished are a-one in death:
Coward and brave: friend, foe. Ghosts do not say,
"Come, what was your record when you drew breath?"

But a big blot has hid each yesterday
So poor, so manifestly incomplete.
And your bright Promise, withered long and sped,
Is touched, stirs, rises, opens and grows sweet
And blossoms and is you, when you are dead.

When You See Millions of the Mouthless Dead

When you see millions of the mouthless dead

Across your dreams in pale battalions go,

Say not soft things as other men have said,

That you'll remember. For you need not so.

Give them not praise. For, deaf, how should they know

It is not curses heaped on each gashed head?

Nor tears. Their blind eyes see not your tears flow.

Nor honour. It is easy to be dead.

Say only this, "They are dead." Then add thereto,

"Yet many a better one has died before."

Then, scanning all the o'ercrowded mass, should you

Perceive one face that you loved heretofore,

It is a spook. None wears the face you knew.

Great death has made all his for evermore.

Robert Graves

A Dead Boche

To you who'd read my songs of War

And only hear of blood and fame,

I'll say (you've heard it said before)

"War's Hell!" and if you doubt the same,

Today I found in Mametz Wood

A certain cure for lust of blood:

Where, propped against a shattered trunk,

In a great mess of things unclean,

Sat a dead Boche; he scowled and stunk

With clothes and face a sodden green,

Big-bellied, spectacled, crop-haired,

Dribbling black blood from nose and beard.

Cecil Day–Lewis

The Volunteer

Tell them in England, if they ask
What brought us to these wars,
To this plateau beneath the night's
Grave manifold of stars –

It was not fraud or foolishness,
Glory, revenge, or pay:
We came because our open eyes
Could see no other way.

There was no other way to keep
Man's flickering truth alight:
These stars will witness that our course
Burned briefer, not less bright.

Beyond the wasted olive-groves,
The furthest lift of land,
There calls a country that was ours
And here shall be regained.

Shine on us, memoried and real,

Green-water-silken meads:

Rivers of home, refresh our path

Whom here your influence leads.

Here in a parched and stranger place

We fight for England free,

The good our fathers won for her,

The land they hoped to see.

John Betjeman

Slough

Come friendly bombs and fall on Slough!

It isn't fit for humans now,

There isn't grass to graze a cow.

Swarm over, Death!

Come, bombs and blow to smithereens

Those air-conditioned, bright canteens,

Tinned fruit, tinned meat, tinned milk, tinned beans,

Tinned minds, tinned breath.

Mess up the mess they call a town—

A house for ninety-seven down

And once a week a half a crown

For twenty years.

And get that man with double chin

Who'll always cheat and always win,

Who washes his repulsive skin

In women's tears:

And smash his desk of polished oak

And smash his hands so used to stroke

And stop his boring dirty joke

And make him yell.

But spare the bald young clerks who add

The profits of the stinking cad;

It's not their fault that they are mad,

They've tasted Hell.

It's not their fault they do not know

The birdsong from the radio,

It's not their fault they often go

To Maidenhead

And talk of sport and makes of cars

In various bogus-Tudor bars

And daren't look up and see the stars

But belch instead.

In labour-saving homes, with care

Their wives frizz out peroxide hair

And dry it in synthetic air

And paint their nails.

Come, friendly bombs and fall on Slough

To get it ready for the plough.

The cabbages are coming now;

The earth exhales.

In Westminster Abbey

Let me take this other glove off

As the vox humana swells,
And the beauteous fields of Eden
Bask beneath the Abbey bells.
Here, where England's statesmen lie,
Listen to a lady's cry.

Gracious Lord, oh bomb the Germans,
Spare their women for Thy Sake,
And if that is not too easy
We will pardon Thy Mistake.
But, gracious Lord, whate'er shall be,
Don't let anyone bomb me.

Keep our Empire undismembered
Guide our Forces by Thy Hand,
Gallant blacks from far Jamaica,
Honduras and Togoland;
Protect them Lord in all their fights,
And, even more, protect the whites.

Think of what our Nation stands for,
Books from Boots' and country lanes,
Free speech, free passes, class distinction,
Democracy and proper drains.

Lord, put beneath Thy special care
One-eighty-nine Cadogan Square.

Although dear Lord I am a sinner,
I have done no major crime;
Now I'll come to Evening Service
Whensoever I have the time.
So, Lord, reserve for me a crown,
And do not let my shares go down.

I will labour for Thy Kingdom,
Help our lads to win the war,
Send white feathers to the cowards
Join the Women's Army Corps,
Then wash the steps around Thy Throne

In the Eternal Safety Zone.
Now I feel a little better,
What a treat to hear Thy Word,
Where the bones of leading statesmen
Have so often been interr'd.
And now, dear Lord, I cannot wait
Because I have a luncheon date.

Wystan Hugh Auden

Epitaph for the Unknown Soldier

To save your world you asked this man to die:
Would this man, could he see you now, ask why?

The Shield of Achilles

   She looked over his shoulder
      For vines and olive trees,
   Marble well-governed cities
      And ships upon untamed seas,
   But there on the shining metal
      His hands had put instead
   An artificial wilderness
      And a sky like lead.

A plain without a feature, bare and brown,
   No blade of grass, no sign of neighborhood,
Nothing to eat and nowhere to sit down,
   Yet, congregated on its blankness, stood
      An unintelligible multitude,
A million eyes, a million boots in line,

Without expression, waiting for a sign.

Out of the air a voice without a face
   Proved by statistics that some cause was just
In tones as dry and level as the place:
   No one was cheered and nothing was discussed;
   Column by column in a cloud of dust
They marched away enduring a belief
Whose logic brought them, somewhere else, to grief.

She looked over his shoulder
   For ritual pieties,
White flower-garlanded heifers,
   Libation and sacrifice,
But there on the shining metal
   Where the altar should have been,
She saw by his flickering forge-light
   Quite another scene.

Barbed wire enclosed an arbitrary spot
   Where bored officials lounged (one cracked a joke)
And sentries sweated for the day was hot:
   A crowd of ordinary decent folk
   Watched from without and neither moved nor spoke

As three pale figures were led forth and bound
To three posts driven upright in the ground.

The mass and majesty of this world, all
    That carries weight and always weighs the same
Lay in the hands of others; they were small
    And could not hope for help and no help came:
    What their foes like to do was done, their shame
Was all the worst could wish; they lost their pride
And died as men before their bodies died.

    She looked over his shoulder
        For athletes at their games,
    Men and women in a dance
        Moving their sweet limbs
    Quick, quick, to music,
        But there on the shining shield
    His hands had set no dancing-floor
        But a weed-choked field.

A ragged urchin, aimless and alone,
    Loitered about that vacancy; a bird
Flew up to safety from his well-aimed stone:
    That girls are raped, that two boys knife a third,

Were axioms to him, who'd never heard
Of any world where promises were kept,
Or one could weep because another wept.

    The thin-lipped armorer,
        Hephaestos, hobbled away,
    Thetis of the shining breasts
        Cried out in dismay
    At what the god had wrought
        To please her son, the strong
    Iron-hearted man-slaying Achilles
        Who would not live long.

Clifford Dyment

The Son

I found the letter in a cardboard box,

Unfamous history. I read the words.

The ink was frail and brown, the paper dry

After so many years of being kept.

The letter was a soldier's, from the front—

Conveyed his love and disappointed hope

Of getting leave. It's cancelled now, he wrote.

My luck is at the bottom of the sea.

Outside the sun was hot; the world looked bright;

I heard a radio, and someone laughed.

I did not sing, or laugh, or love the sun,

Within the quiet room I thought of him,

My father killed, and all the other men,

Whose luck was at the bottom of the sea.

Dylan Thomas

The Hand That Signed the Paper

The hand that signed the paper felled a city;
Five sovereign fingers taxed the breath,
Doubled the globe of dead and halved a country;
These five kings did a king to death.

The mighty hand leads to a sloping shoulder,
The finger joints are cramped with chalk;
A goose's quill has put an end to murder
That put an end to talk.

The hand that signed the treaty bred a fever,
And famine grew, and locusts came;
Great is the hand that holds dominion over
Man by a scribbled name.

The five kings count the dead but do not soften
The crusted wound nor pat the brow;
A hand rules pity as a hand rules heaven;
Hands have no tears to flow.

Eve Merriam

The Coward

You, weeping wide at war, weep with me now.

Cheating a little at peace, come near

And let us cheat together here.

Look at my guilt, mirror of my shame.

Deserter, I will not turn you in;

I am your trembling twin!

Afraid, our double knees lock in knocking fear;

Running from the guns we stumble upon each other.

Hide in my lap of terror: I am your mother.

— Only we two, and yet our howling can

Encircle the world's end.

Frightened, you are my only friend.

And frightened, we are everyone.

Someone must make a stand.

Coward, take my coward's hand.

John Lennon

Imagine

Imagine there's no heaven

It's easy if you try

No hell below us

Above us, only sky

Imagine all the people

Living for today ...

Imagine there's no countries

It isn't hard to do

Nothing to kill or die for

And no religion too

Imagine all the people

Living life in peace ...

You may say I'm a dreamer

But I'm not the only one

I hope someday you'll join us

And the world will be as one

Imagine no possessions

I wonder if you can

No need for greed or hunger

A brotherhood of man

Imagine all the people

Sharing all the world ...

You may say I'm a dreamer

But I'm not the only one

I hope someday you'll join us

And the world will live as one

Give Peace a Chance

Two, one-two-three-four!

Ev'rybody's talking 'bout

Bagism, Shagism, Dragism, Madism, Ragism, Tagism

This-ism, that-ism, is-m, is-m, is-m

All we are saying is give peace a chance

All we are saying is give peace a chance

C'mon, ev'rybody's talking about

Ministers, sinisters, banisters and canisters

Bishops and Fishops and Rabbis and Popeyes and bye-bye, bye-byes

All we are saying is give peace a chance
All we are saying is give peace a chance

Let me tell you now
Ev'rybody's talking 'bout
Revolution, evolution, masturbation, flagellation, regulation,
 integrations
Meditations, United Nations, congratulations

All we are saying is give peace a chance
All we are saying is give peace a chance

Ev'rybody's talking 'bout
John and Yoko, Timmy Leary, Rosemary, Tommy Smothers,
Bobby Dylan, Tommy Cooper
Derek Taylor, Norman Mailer, Alan Ginsberg, Hare Krishna, Hare,
Hare Krishna

All we are saying is give peace a chance
All we are saying is give peace a chance

All we are saying is give peace a chance
All we are saying is give peace a chance

All we are saying is give peace a chance

All we are saying is give peace a chance

All we are saying is give peace a chance

All we are saying is give peace a chance

All we are saying is give peace a chance

All we are saying is give peace a chance

All we are saying is give peace a chance

All we are saying is give peace a chance

All we are saying is give peace a chance

David Krieger

The Children of Iraq Have Names

The children of Iraq have names.
They are not the nameless ones.

The children of Iraq have faces.
They are not the faceless ones.

The children of Iraq do not wear Saddam's face.
They each have their own face.

The children of Iraq have names.
They are not all called Saddam Hussein.

The children of Iraq have hearts.
They are not the heartless ones.

The children of Iraq have dreams.
They are not the dreamless ones.

The children of Iraq have hearts that pound.
They are not meant to be statistics of war.

The children of Iraq have smiles.
They are not the sullen ones.

The children of Iraq have twinkling eyes.
They are quick and lively with their laughter.

The children of Iraq have hopes.
They are not the hopeless ones.

The children of Iraq have fears.
They are not the fearless ones.

The children of Iraq have names.
Their names are not collateral damage.

What do you call the children of Iraq?
Call them Omar, Mohamed, Fahad.

Call them Marwa and Tiba.
Call them by their names.

But never call them statistics of war.
Never call them collateral damage.

Worse Than the War

Worse than the war, the endless, senseless war,
Worse than the lies leading to the war,

Worse than the countless deaths and injuries,
Worse than hiding the coffins and not attending funerals,

Worse than the flouting of international law,
Worse than the torture at Abu Ghraib prison,

Worse than the corruption of young soldiers,
Worse than undermining our collective sense of decency,

Worse than the arrogance, smugness and swagger,
Worse than our loss of credibility in the world,
Worse than the loss of our liberties,

Worse than learning nothing from the past,
Worse than destroying the future,
Worse than the incredible stupidity of it all,

Worse than all of these,
As if they were not enough for one war or country or lifetime,
Is the silence, the resounding silence of good Americans.

To an Iraqi Child
for Ali Ismail Abbas

So you wanted to be a doctor?

It was not likely that your dreams
would have come true anyway.

We didn't intend for our bombs to find you.

They are smart bombs, but they didn't know
that you wanted to be a doctor.

They didn't know anything about you
and they know nothing of love.

They cannot be trusted with dreams.

They only know how to find their targets
and explode in fulfillment.

They are gray metal casings with violent hearts,
doing only what they were created to do.

It isn't their fault that they found you.

Perhaps you were not meant to be a doctor.

Greeting Bush in Baghdad

"This is a farewell kiss, you dog."

— Muntader al-Zaidi

You are a guest in my country, unwanted

surely, but still a guest.

You stand before us waiting for praise,

but how can we praise you?

You come after your planes have rained

death on our cities.

Your soldiers broke down our doors,

humiliated our men, disgraced our women.

We are not a frontier town and you are not

our marshal.

You are a torturer. We know you force water
down the throats of our prisoners.

We have seen the pictures of our naked prisoners
threatened by your snarling dogs.

You are a maker of widows and orphans,
a most unwelcome guest.

I have only this for you, my left shoe that I hurl
at your lost and smirking face,

and my right shoe that I throw at your face
of no remorse.

Zaid's Misfortune

Zaid had the misfortune
of being born in Iraq, a country
rich with oil.

Iraq had the misfortune
of being invaded by a country
greedy for oil.

The country greedy for oil
had the misfortune of being led
by a man too eager for war.

Zaid's misfortune multiplied
when his parents were shot down
in front of their medical clinic.

Being eleven and haunted
by the deaths of one's parents
is a great misfortune.

In Zaid's misfortune
a distant silence engulfs
the sounds of war.

Andrew Motion

The Death of Harry Patch

When the next morning eventually breaks,
a young Captain climbs onto the fire step,
knocks ash from his pipe then drops it
still warm into his pocket, checks his watch,
and places the whistle back between his lips.
At 06.00 hours precisely he gives the signal,
but today nothing that happens next happens
according to plan. A very long and gentle note
wanders away from him over the ruined ground
and hundreds of thousands of dead who lie there
immediately rise up, straightening their tunics
before falling in as they used to do, shoulder
shoulder, eyes front. They have left a space
for the last recruit of all to join them: Harry Patch,
one hundred and eleven years old, but this is him
now, running quick-sharp along the duckboards.
When he has taken his place, and the whole company
are settled at last, their padre appears out of nowhere,
pausing a moment in front of each and every one
to slip a wafer of dry mud onto their tongues.

Regime Change

Advancing down the road from Nineveh

Death paused a while and said 'Now listen here.

You see the names of places roundabout?

They're mine now, and I've turned them inside out.

Take Eden, further south: At dawn today

I ordered up my troops to tear away

Its walls and gates so everyone can see

That gorgeous fruit which dangles from its tree.

You want it, don't you? Go and eat it then,

and lick your lips, and pick the same again.

Take Tigris and Euphrates; once they ran

Through childhood-coloured slats of sand and sun.

Not any more they don't; I've filled them up

With countless different kinds of human crap.

Take Babylon, the palace sprouting flowers

Which sweetened empires in their peaceful hours —

I've found a different way to scent the air:
Already it's a by-word for despair.

Which leaves Baghdad - the star-tipped minarets,
The marble courts and halls, the mirage-heat.

These places, and the ancient things you know,
You won't know soon. I'm working on it now.'

译后记

战争伴随着人类历史的发展进程。对战争的书写也是文学、诗歌的重要组成部分。

《英语战争诗歌选》跨越时空，涉及了18世纪的西班牙王位战争，19世纪的克里米亚战争、美国内战，20世纪的布尔战争、西班牙内战、两次世界大战、越南战争，直至21世纪的伊拉克战争。

本诗选收录了英语诗坛40余位诗人的近百首诗歌。有因第一次世界大战而诞生的特殊群体——战争诗人的杰出代表约翰·麦克雷、爱德华·托马斯、西格弗里德·萨松、鲁伯特·布鲁克、艾萨克·罗森伯格、威尔弗雷德·欧文、查尔斯·汉密尔顿·索利等的战争诗歌。还有英语世界的伟大诗人，诸如英国桂冠诗人骚塞、丁尼生、刘易斯、莫伸，获得诺贝尔文学奖的吉卜林、叶芝，"悖论王子"切斯特顿，对英国文学乃至世界文学产生深远影响的哈代，传奇诗人狄兰·托马斯，拥有"20世纪最伟大思想"的W.H.奥登，和美国现代诗歌的杰出代表自由诗之父惠特曼，意象派诗歌的奠基人庞德，被称为"美国之声"的卡尔·桑德堡，美国20世纪最受敬仰的诗人之一华莱士·史蒂文斯，及多次获得诺贝尔和平奖提名的美国当代诗人大卫·克里格等关于战争的诗篇。本诗选还收录了艾米莉·狄金森、凯瑟琳·泰南、萨拉·蒂斯代尔 等女性诗人以独特、细腻的视角抒写的战争诗歌。本书所选战争诗歌既有弘扬爱国主义的战争诗篇，也有痛斥战争的批判现实主义的反战诗篇。

《英语战争诗歌选》最终得以出炉，首先要感谢西安电子科技大学外国语学院领导及学院经费上的鼎力支持。

感谢一如既往支持我的英国剑桥博学家Martin John Bishop教授，正是因为他的无私帮助——有问必答，我才有了将自己的想法变为现实的勇气和底气，我坚信他就是上天派来的救兵。

感谢英国当代著名女诗人温迪·蔻普（Wendy Cope）和其丈夫——英国当代诗人Lachlan Mackinnon为我答疑解惑了本书中爱德华·托马斯诗歌中的晦涩词句。

感谢大卫·克里格的遗孀Carolee Krieger，让我免费使用本书中其丈夫针对伊拉克战争的诗作；感谢她邮件中温暖、鼓励的话语。感谢普林斯顿大学的荣誉退休教授Richard Falk为我搭建的联络桥梁。

特别感谢西安外国语大学的汉语教授张丽娜老师于百忙中耐心专业的指点，一些表达，被她首肯，我似乎才觉得踏实。

最后，感谢为本书作出贡献的我的弟子们——西安电子科技大学外国语学院的学生陈韵姿、刘豆豆、石佳凝、王莹莹、张慧珂，感谢她们的辛苦付出！

即使有专家的挚诚相助，有专业人士的悉心指点，但每每将铅字作品捧在手上，总发现有不尽人意的地方，遗憾有之，懊恼有之，相信此诗选也概莫能外。还是那句老话，有最佳的作品，没有最佳的译著。不足之处，恳请专家、同仁、读者海涵。

徐艳萍

2024年9月于西电南校区